SAME TIME
NEXT WEEK

By the Author

Searching for Forever

Same Time Next Week

SAME TIME NEXT WEEK

by
Emily Smith

2015

SAME TIME NEXT WEEK
© 2015 By Emily Smith. All Rights Reserved.

ISBN 13: 978-1-62639-345-5

This Trade Paperback Original Is Published By
Bold Strokes Books, Inc.
P.O. Box 249
Valley Falls, NY 12185

First Edition: May 2015

Credits
Editor: Shelley Thrasher
Production Design: Stacia Seaman
Cover Design by Gabrielle Pendergrast

To Jillian—thanks for being my happily-ever-after

PROLOGUE

I'm a cliché, sitting in a coffee shop surrounded by dykes, reading stories from *The Best Lesbian Romance*, still in tattered paperback while I'm immersed in a sea of e-readers and computers. The women here are all cooler than me, each emanating her own sort of hipster vibe, complete with thick-rimmed glasses and wool caps that have nothing to do with the warm spring air outside. They're cooler, yes, and at almost thirty, they also seem to be about a century younger than I am as well. I haven't been here since I broke up with Tory—also known as the most insignificant relationship in the history of the lesbian world. And not since Beth and I have been married, either.

Married—what a ridiculous concept. I didn't *feel* married. No. I still feel very much the same twenty-three-year-old bachelor who used to break hearts left and right when I was bored or ready to move on to the next endeavor. And yet, I'm not breaking hearts anymore. At least not yet.

What I remember most about my wedding to Beth is the heat. It was ninety-five degrees on the shores of the gay mecca of Provincetown, and the sea breeze was doing absolutely nothing to relieve the film of sweat forming under my white dress shirt. I waited with my "groomsmen," a bunch of butches in black Dockers, trying to keep my heart rate from taking off. And, as I stood in front of Beth, all my focus went into staying conscious. Your wedding day should be about fantasy and romance and happily-ever-after. And maybe ours was. But somehow, over the years, "happily-ever-after" has turned to "for as long as we can stand it."

But it's becoming harder and harder to stand it. I'm getting restless, and at a rate much faster than I'd ever imagined. When I proposed, on Christmas Day, Beth and I had only been dating for about eight months. Her mother, who loved me, was thrilled that we'd decided to settle down, and even more thrilled that I'd picked her daughter. Her father, a rough-and-tumble blue-collar type, had his share of reservations. But when I broke out the tiny, half-caret ring, and she said yes, and I cried, none of that mattered. I cried big sloppy tears. Tears that seemed to say, "You're doing the right thing, Alex." Tears don't mean shit.

When she walks in, I'm three pages deep into a story about a carpenter who seduces a single mother. She's tall, with long, flowing chestnut hair that bounces against her back as she makes her way toward the table for two I'm occupying.

"Do you mind?" she asks, plainly, gesturing to the empty seat across from me. "It's pretty full in here."

"Of course not." I stare at her for at least thirty awkward seconds before she eyes the cover of my open book. "I'm a lawyer," I say, defensively, as if that should somehow excuse the pleasure reading on my table.

"I'm Michelle."

CHAPTER ONE

When I interviewed for law school, almost seven years ago now, the dean of the university asked me to tell him about the moment I knew I wanted to be a lawyer. I gave some practiced answer about legal injustice in Syria I'd loosely based on a *Dateline* episode, but the truth of it was, I'd had no such moment. Life is so rarely defined in single days or events we can pinpoint—those *aha* moments that are supposed to change everything. But *that* day—the day I met Michelle— that was one of them.

❖

I found myself back in the town's dyke-run coffee shop for the second time that week. It was Saturday, and I'd told my wife, Beth, I needed to get some work done on a case involving an old lady who'd slipped on some Red Bull in a Walmart. If I didn't, I told her, I'd never make partner. We both knew the only partnership I'd be making anytime soon was the one I formed with the barista at the Starbucks who filled the office coffee orders for me. Besides, this place was full of loud, teenage (well, teenage to me) hipster lesbians who chatted wildly about dates and parties and feminism while they sipped mochaccinos by the pool tables. I didn't know exactly what I was doing there again. But working on Eleanor Cohen's Red Bull case certainly wasn't it.

I hadn't been able to stop thinking about the girl from earlier in the week. It was true, it definitely wasn't the first time I'd occupied myself by contemplating the way someone else's hips swung or lips moved. More often than I liked to admit, those were the things that got me through my marriage. But this one, Michelle, she stayed with me, offering more than just a momentary distraction from my blistering relationship.

Michelle walked in at 2:15 p.m., wearing a flowing purple blouse I couldn't help but notice fell just below the top of her breasts. A wool pencil skirt hugged her curvy hips and straight waist, and a pair of black pumps made her even taller than the last time I'd seen her, which was really also the first time I'd seen her. She must have caught my stare, because she offered a small smile and made her way through the crowd and toward my table for two.

"No book today?" She pulled out the mismatched red chair across from me.

"Not today," I said with a smile, hoping to regain just a modicum of the charisma I knew I'd had only a few years ago. Back then, I could charm my way into just about anyone's pants. I had all the right lines, the right moves. Then again, I was also a complete jackass. I guess I'd traded some of my machismo in for just a hint of chivalry. "I'm working today."

"Working on a Saturday?" Without asking, she grabbed the manila folder in front of me marked CONFIDENTIAL and opened it.

"That's um…"

"Confidential? Yes, I can read too." She peeked over the folder at me, her eyes bright and confident, and something inside me woke up.

❖

I went back on Tuesday, biking the four blocks from the firm in hopes of running into her again.

Michelle was later than she had been on Saturday, and I looked for her every minute after 2:15, as if her stylish Banana Republic attire had to mean she was the kind of girl to keep a strict coffee schedule. What made me think she'd even be back? Hell, even I could count the number of times I'd been there on one hand. For all I knew about her, she was an out-of-towner, visiting a sister or cousin, accidentally stumbling into the gayest Northwood establishment in search of a decent cup of coffee. Stupid. And what would I do if she did come back, anyway? The ring on my left hand was the heavy anchor that kept me from going too far out to sea. Things with Beth had been rough for longer than I could remember. Maybe I was just lonely.

I was already halfway through my designated lunch break, chewing mindlessly at the last bite of my bagel as I stared at the door, when she finally entered. This time, she was draped in hospital scrubs, a purple stethoscope swinging from her neck.

I fought the almost visceral urge to jump out of my seat and wave like an idiot, but she was already making her way to me.

"You aren't going to pull my chair out for me? Huh. I took you for a gentleman," she said, sitting down next to me.

"I…uh…"

"Oh, Alex. You know you're awfully cute when you're nervous."

Flirting. For the last few years, I wasn't even sure I'd have recognized it, never mind known what to do with it. But there it was. As blatant as the dumbfounded grin that took over my face when she said my name. For twenty-eight years I'd been Alex, or Al, or Allie Wallie (that one was Mom and her bridge buddies), but never once had I heard my name sound quite like that. When Michelle used it, especially that first time, it was like hearing a new language. One reserved only for me. One that made my cheeks burn and my palms sweat.

"So, you're a lawyer?" *Okay, let's see if the third attempt to answer her is a charm.*

"Yes. Well…technically."

"Meaning?"

"Meaning," I said, regaining some version of the confidence that usually came readily to me, "I'm sort of a paralegal right now. I passed the bar and everything. But the job market…"

"Don't worry about it. I have a friend who passed the bar and is selling perfume at Macy's. You're young. Plenty of time."

"How young do you think I am?"

"Young enough that it's completely acceptable you're still doing sandwich runs for middle-aged men with comb-overs." She flashed her beautiful white teeth at me. Beth's teeth were always a little crooked. "But old enough to be married." She ran her thumb across the gold wedding band on my hand. The anchor.

"Debatable," I mumbled.

My marriage wasn't something I usually enjoyed discussing with complete strangers. Or at all, actually. Even if this one did make a pair of scrub pants look like a patient's wet dream.

"Oh, please. You butch lesbians are all alike. Can't commit even when there's a ring on your finger."

"That's an awful big generalization, seeing as you hardly know me." But there was nothing cold in my tone.

"Do you love her?" Even her tactlessness was sort of adorable.

"I married her, didn't I?"

"That's not an answer."

❖

"Beth? I'm home." Our dreary apartment was exactly that—dreary. Three days' worth of dirty dishes were stacked in and around the kitchen sink, so many you wouldn't believe just the two of us lived there. The overhead light fixture was too dim, several of the bulbs needing to be replaced. The tiled floor had collected more than a few weeks' worth of dirt and dust balls and a clutter of unopened junk mail, and empty cereal boxes took over the counter.

Jed, Beth's Maine Coon, met me at the door like he did every day, purring and rubbing his massive frame against my shins.

"Hey, Big Guy." I reached down to scratch the spot right at the base of his tail, where he loved to be touched so much.

"Hi." Beth emerged from the bedroom, dressed in the same oversized UCLA sweatshirt, *my* UCLA sweatshirt, and yoga pants she always wore, looking very much like every day of my life. We had so many nights like this. So many evenings where I came through that same door into that same dreary kitchen, with the same overweight cat rubbing against my shins, and the same wife, in the same UCLA sweatshirt. Three years into married life, and everything was the same.

"Hey." She walked casually to me and put her arms around my neck. I could smell her perfume—the same one she'd worn for the last four years. It was the same perfume that had set me on fire when we first got together. I don't remember a lot of depth or substance with Beth in the beginning, but I do remember a lot of heat. More than once, we had to sneak off to a bathroom or a dark corner just to get at each other. But that didn't last long either. It became the same perfume that, a year in, comforted me, offering me solace and friendship and a rock to rest on when I couldn't stand on my own. And it was the same perfume, now, that made me cringe, just slightly, a reminder of slowly being crushed under the weight of my own choices.

"What do you want for dinner?" I obliged her by putting my hands on her hips, but it had been a long time since touching Beth had felt good. We went through the motions, like always, but the passion behind them had begun to slip away.

"Anything."

"I'll put together some tacos." I was no cook, that was for sure. All through college, I'd survived on food from the university dining hall, the late-night frozen yogurt stand down the street, and whatever girl I was dating who was somehow able, and willing, to feed me. My wife, however, was not one of those girls. Her culinary expertise fell somewhere between boxed macaroni and cheese and scrambled eggs, and more often than not, we found ourselves eating whatever leftovers she'd brought back from the bar the night before.

Three years ago, when I slipped that chintzy wedding band on Beth's left hand, I didn't know what married life would look like. I knew I'd have a lot to learn. What I never imagined, though, was feeling so much like a couple of kids playing house.

Chapter Two

On Saturday, I biked down Lincoln, the spring thaw biting my nose. Michelle was already inside, sitting at the counter this time. A pair of black reading glasses, not altogether different from those the café hipsters around us wore, rested on her nose as she typed furiously on a laptop in front of her.

"Is this seat taken?" I asked quietly, edging closer to her but never touching.

"You're so cheesy." Michelle looked up from her work, her perfect cheekbones just slightly more pink than I'd seen them before. She pulled out the stool next to her and I sat down.

"If you're busy, I can—"

"No." She jumped up and grabbed my arm. "Stay. Please."

I ordered a small black coffee and a bagel with jam from the blond, spiky-haired girl behind the counter and took out Eleanor's case file.

"Still working on that Red Bull case?"

"Yeah. Right now I'm going through all the slip-and-fall data from every Walmart in the county in the last three years. Invigorating." I liked that she asked about my work. Beth never seemed to take much interest in what happened during my day. Somewhere along the line, we'd just stopped talking about it. "What about you? What are you working on?"

Michelle silently turned her laptop screen, revealing a beautiful image of a park with the words SAVE OUR GREEN SPACE scrawled on top.

"But on Tuesday you were here in scrubs..." I said, the confusion surely evident on my face.

"This is my part-time gig. I work for the county parks department, saving the world one tree at a time."

"And your other gig?"

She smiled with her full lips that wore red when she wasn't coming from whatever her day job was.

"Nurse. I work over at Northwood Hospital. In the Emergency Room."

"So you're like...some kind of superhero then?"

She chuckled, and I swore I saw the red rise across her smooth, white skin.

"Something like that."

"Impressive," I said, meaning it.

Beth was younger than me, which, I guess, in some obscure way, made it acceptable for her to be a bartender with little to no ambition to be more. For almost four years, I'd told myself this was fine. She was just figuring out what she wanted. Anyway, who was I to judge, besides a pencil pusher and latte retriever for Watson, Johnson and Smith? But as Michelle talked about her work—her passion for saving her patients or saving the planet—it became harder to deny that these things that I once told myself didn't matter. Well, they did.

❖

Michelle and I met like this twice a week for a month, eventually giving up the facade of just bumping into one another. It had become intentional. Incredibly intentional, really. At least on my end. I lay awake at night next to Beth's ignorant snoring, imagining what Michelle's lips would feel like against mine. I fantasized about faint lip gloss and light, musky perfume and handfuls of her silky blouses in my hands. A month of over-caffeinated conversation, and I still didn't even know if Michelle had a girlfriend. Or, worse, a boyfriend, maybe? But the way she looked at me told me she probably didn't. Not that it really mattered if she was available. For better or worse, I was not. As sordid as things had gotten between Beth and me, these were just harmless fantasies.

These coffee dates (which I could neither reasonably nor morally call "dates"), with this girl, this stranger, were breathing life into something I didn't know was dead. They were breathing life into *me*. I was waking up in the morning thinking about her and going to bed counting down the days until Tuesday, or Saturday, when I would walk into the café and not-so-accidentally find her sitting at the counter, reading a weathered copy of J.D. Salinger or a borrowed Michael Crichton novel, depending on the mood she was in. I quickly found myself, only somewhat inadvertently, memorizing her routine; Tuesdays meant scrubs from the end of an early morning shift and an extra-large Colombian roast with one Splenda. Saturdays always brought out those Coke-bottle reading glasses and an Earl Grey tea.

Beth and I had been married for three years, and I still couldn't tell you how she took her coffee. And I don't think she could tell you how I took mine either.

❖

"Tell me about your wife," Michelle asked on another long Tuesday lunch break.

"My wife? But why?"

"I want to know what kind of woman it took to lock you down." She reached out and touched my wedding band again.

I didn't know her well. After all, how much can you know about somebody you only share a latte with twice a week? But something told me Michelle wasn't shy. Ambitious, warm-hearted, yes. Shy? Not a chance in hell. And when she touched me like that, offered me little tokens of affection that really couldn't be taken as much more than that, I had to wonder if she was like this with others—if a particularly outgoing persona was often mistaken for purposeful flirtation—or if she was really interested in me. Then I'd quietly remind myself it didn't matter how interested Michelle was. I was married. Maybe if I kept repeating that fact, it'd mean more than it did.

"She's twenty-five. She tends bar at the Applebee's down the street. She's…" I froze. Was I that incapable of finding a few nice things to say about Beth? It wasn't always that way. In the first couple of years, I gushed about her to everyone I met. Beth didn't have a shiny degree or a high-paying job or anything that contributed to what society considered "status." But she had passion, for life and for me. She showed it in everything she said and did. Beth had one of those rare, oversized hearts that was capable of all kinds of love. She made people laugh. She made me laugh. *No, it wasn't always this way*.

"Glowing review." Michelle was teasing me. "How long have you been married?"

"About three years now."

"Three blissful years, I see?" She loved poking fun at me. I was almost certain she was getting some kind of thrill from the color draining out of my face.

"Marriage is hard," I replied matter-of-factly.

It was hard. It was much fucking harder than anyone ever tells you. When I told my parents I was getting married, my mother said to me, "Divorce is expensive, Alex." Pearls of wisdom coming from the woman with four husbands. *I'll never make your mistakes*, I'd grumble to myself. If only I'd had any idea I was about to marry someone for mostly the wrong reasons. I was already making her mistakes.

"Do you regret it?" she asked. I thought about staying the course of denial. But something in the candid way Michelle looked at me told me I didn't have to.

"Sometimes." I thought about Beth—about my wife.

I thought about how, when I was twenty-five myself, she was going to be enough for me. Our life was going to be enough for me. We had been best friends for years before we got together. Or, rather, she was my best friend. I was the object of her undying affection.

My cousin had introduced us without any real intent, on a weekend at the end of the summer I graduated from law school. She was young (although, so was I back then), and full of that adventurous breath that made you feel like you were absolutely missing out on something she was in on. Beth was down for anything and never up before noon. She long-boarded down Main Street in her bra and panties, with only a little help from a few Coors, still hung out with the kids who would have made fun of me in high school, and never, for a second, seemed to doubt she could do anything. I was a magna cum laude UCLA graduate, living in her parents' attic for the summer, studying for the bar and going to bed after Letterman. In a matter of a weekend, Beth made me feel the way twenty-three-year-olds were supposed to. And, by the end of the weekend, when she hurled herself at me for a dorm-room-hookup-worthy kiss, she made me feel wanted too. Beth ignored the fact I was still in a year-long relationship with a girl back in California. But that was college. And everything was changing, anyway.

In the beginning, I loved the way Beth loved me. It was strong and seemingly endless. No matter who I'd been with, or what I'd done, she was right there, ready to forgive me— ready to take me in her arms. And I grew to love her for that strength and resilience. I should have known that would never be enough, though. Not for either of us.

❖

A month of talking about the theater, and the most recent exhibit at the city museum, and the rose garden in the park she took care of, and Michelle had morphed into the archetype of everything I'd ever known I wanted in a girl but was too afraid to ask for. She felt it too. I knew it when she'd lightly touch my arm or brush by me to get to her seat at the counter. I knew it when she started getting to the café early, with my bagel and jam and black coffee waiting for me. I knew it when she stopped asking about Beth as often. Two days a week, I was able to escape the shambles my home life had deteriorated into and spend time with someone who was interested in knowing me. Beth and I hadn't seemed to know each other for a while now.

It was just coffee, though. A little detour from the drudgery of my marriage. I wasn't brave enough, or maybe foolish enough, to make it more than that. Somehow, though, what little it was had become enough to sustain me.

CHAPTER THREE

It's getting late. I should head out," I said, and sighed. It was Saturday. Spring was in full bloom in Rhode Island and everything felt a little easier. I took my dirty plate to the buckets in the front of the café and returned back to grab my coat.

"Me too." Michelle got up from her chair, carefully wrapped a purple silk scarf around her neck, and leaned in as if to hug me. I did the same, though much faster, bumping her forehead with mine in a freakishly middle-school snafu. "Sorry I…"

"No, that one's on me." We smiled shyly and walked out the door, together, into the warm afternoon.

It normally took seventeen minutes to bike home, but I took my time riding down the winding streets, reveling in the feeling of the breeze against my skin. The light rain pelted my face as I rode.

"Have you been at the coffee shop this whole time?" Beth quietly questioned me as I opened the front door to our apartment and attempted to brush the wet from my denim coat. I pulled the Red Sox cap off my head, never bothering to look at her.

"Yes."

"Doing what?"

"You know what. I was working," I replied simply.

"The whole time?"

"Yes, Beth. The whole time."

She came in to kiss me, a gesture that had become increasingly mechanical as time passed, and I returned the motion. "Well, I'm glad you're home. I have to leave for the bar in an hour."

"I'm going to order a pizza for dinner. Sound okay?"

"Sure."

Beth ran off to shower and get ready for work, and I was alone again, relieved by the reprieve. I was always a little relieved when she left now. I called in for delivery, searching my coat pockets for my credit card with the phone wedged between my chin and my shoulder. I didn't find the credit card. But I did find a fresh piece of stiff paper tucked in next to my keys.

Michelle M Masters
Rhode Island Parks Commission
Fundraising Director 555-2495

"Hello? Ma'am? What can I get you?"

"What?"

"Your pizza? What would you like?"

"Oh God, I'm sorry. Uh, just a pepperoni, please."

I turned the card over, the phone still crammed against my ear, not sure what I was looking for.

Six weeks of coffees, I think you owe me a phone call—M

My heart caught in my throat.

"The address?"

"The what?"

"The delivery address, ma'am. We have to have an address to bring you your pizza."

"Oh, right. Of course you do. 132 Brooks Ave. Northwood. Thanks."

I hung up the phone, still holding the business card in a trembling hand.

❖

Thirty minutes later Marco's dropped off our pizza, and Beth and I ate in front of the TV, like we did every night. It had been nearly a year since we'd had dinner at our dining-room table, without the distraction of a Bruins game or a *Simpsons* rerun. We used to talk. Now, the conversation was easy. We never delved into politics or philosophy or our dreams or failures. We specialized in small talk you'd make with a distant friend. I already felt connected to Michelle on a level I didn't to Beth. And that terrified the hell out of me.

"Okay, I have to take off." Relief swam through me as Beth stood from the couch and moved to the door, leaving her empty plate and half cup of Pepsi on the table.

"Have a good shift." I rose, offered her a quick embrace about as heartfelt as the pizza crust on her plate, and she left.

I held Michelle's card for a long time, rubbing it between my thumb and index fingers so long some of the ink began to smudge. My knee bounced up and down, and I stared worthlessly at my cell phone sitting in front of me. Jed, who was perched on the arm of the sofa, looked up at me from his tenth nap that day and glared.

"What? It's just a phone call!" In seeming disbelief, Jed blinked and went back to sleep. I believed that too. I believed, as miserable as Beth and I had become, that I could remain faithful. My vows meant something to me, and I wasn't ready to give up yet.

I picked up the phone, slowly and deliberately punching in each of Michelle's numbers until I reached the last one. I hit the final digit like I was crossing over a land mine that threatened to blow me to tiny pieces at any sign of adultery.

It was ringing.

"Took you longer than I thought." Her smooth, warm voice came through almost as clearly over the phone as it did over coffee.

"It's only been like," I glanced at my watch, "three hours."

"That's two hours and forty-five minutes more than I'd given you credit for. And that's taking into account the time it would take you to get home and find my number."

"What can I say? I'm unpredictable." There was silence on the other end of the line.

"Oh, I'd be willing to bet against that." I could hear her smiling.

"And why is that?"

"I'm willing to bet you don't have the unpredictable balls to come over here and pick me up." I was pretty sure my heart had stopped. "Alex?"

"Huh?"

"Come get me. Let's do something." No. My heart hadn't stopped. If it had, I wouldn't have been able to hear it pounding in my ears.

"I'm married..."

"So? Beth doesn't let you have friends?"

No, Beth didn't let me have friends. At least not attractive female friends who showed any interest in me. Forget interest. They just had to be attractive to set off her radar. The second I mentioned a girl's name she didn't recognize, her face narrowed to a scowl and she went into a sort of attack mode. It didn't matter if it was the girl bagging my groceries who asked for paper of plastic, or Liddy, my very beautiful, but very straight, cubicle buddy. Beth was a force to be reckoned with, and I guessed she'd have more than a few things to say if she even knew Michelle existed. I wasn't sure why she still cared so much. Her jealousy used to be almost endearing, making me feel like some kind of movie star who she was lucky to have on her arm. That feeling had ebbed a while ago, though. I don't think she felt quite so lucky anymore.

"What? Of course she does. Of course I can have friends."

"Then come pick me up." This girl was nothing if not persistent. And I wanted to get in my car and go get her, no matter where she was, no matter what we were doing, more than anything. I just wasn't sure why. "My car's in the shop. I've been walking to work. I live about a mile from Northwood Hospital. You do have a car…don't you?"

I laughed at her, realizing how ridiculous I must seem leaving the café on my little vintage road bike every day.

"Yes, I have a car."

"So then?"

"So then what?"

"Do you, or don't you, have the balls to come see me?"

I paused for what felt like days. And as I did, I thought about all the ways I'd felt trapped lately. I thought about all the times Beth and I had fought about money and our work and our families and anything else that worked its way into our conversation. It seemed we did more fighting lately than laughing. And certainly more than making love. I thought about how it had begun to feel to go home to our dreary one-bedroom with Beth, bitter and resentful. She'd begun to hate the things about me she used to worship—my work ethic, my confidence, my ambition.

I thought about all the times she'd told me "no" in the

recent months: "No, Al, you can't get drinks with the office after work." "No, Al, I don't want to meet your friends." "No, Al, just no." I thought about what it had meant when I took those vows and put on that ring three years back, and I thought about what it meant now. And I felt trapped, chained by some words and a piece of paper and some hunks of metal we wore on our left hands.

"I'll be there."

❖

I didn't know what I was doing. I didn't know where we were going. What I knew was that Beth wouldn't be home for hours, and Michelle's address was scribbled on the pizza receipt in front of me.

My heart raced as I moved to the bedroom and rummaged wildly through the hamper of clean clothes that had yet to be put away. One of Beth's T-shirts, the one with the low V-neck and tiny stain on the hem, had found its way into the pile. I caught it with my hand, studying it like she hadn't worn it four hundred times since I'd known her. Any excitement dissipated into gut-wrenching guilt. And I thought about how I'd gotten here.

I'd had plans. I was going to marry this girl who thought I'd sparked the Big Bang, be a big-shot lawyer, and live a secure, relatively content life with her. But on the day of our wedding, as I read off my cookie-cutter vows about commitment and devotion, and till death do us part, I couldn't shake a tiny feeling that said this would not be "till death do us part." That it would only be "till I snap out of it." It was a selfish voice. The voice of a spoiled child wanting something marked as permanent, knowing full well she would put it back on the shelf if she wanted more. I held her worn T-shirt, thinking there was a part of me, no matter how quiet a part, that always knew this would never be forever. Maybe she did too.

But the guilt ebbed under the pleasure of the unknown as I rushed to put on my favorite navy cotton sweater and jeans. Michelle was a friend. Just a friend. I could keep it at that... Couldn't I?

I don't think I've ever driven so fast in my life. The sun had been down for hours now, and I took the bends in the one-lane highway to Michelle's with so much force my body moved with it. I wanted to get there. I wanted to get there before I could decide not to, before I could decide this was a horrible idea that would absolutely mean the end of my marriage. Beth and I weren't happy anymore. There was no question there. Night after night I came home to her somewhat blank face, where we engaged in shallow, empty conversation, about what I couldn't even tell you. And, although I couldn't deny that Beth was sexy in her own, conventionally collegiate way, I had zero desire for her anymore. It had been more than three months since we'd even attempted to have sex. Eventually, we'd bend to the obligations of marriage and find it in ourselves somewhere to get past just how little seemed to still be between us. It was sad, really. The saddest. But we went on that way, as many lost couples tend to do, scared to death of the alternatives.

I'd raced to Michelle's place like I was trying to escape Armageddon, but when I finally pulled in the driveway, my body seemed stuck to the seat, and I couldn't pry my hands from the steering wheel. A porch light flickered on, and the front door jarred open. She looked like a magazine ad, a long, black raincoat covering her shoulders and contrasting to her chestnut curls that bobbed when she walked.

"Goddamn it. Do you have to be so hot?" I asked both myself and the rain that ran down the windshield of my waiting car. As she approached, I threw open the driver's side door and circled around. She was smiling as I opened it for her.

"That's more like it." She held me with her big, soft eyes for just a second, taking a seat in the passenger side.

"I'm a quick study."

"We'll see about that." Even in the cool air my face burned.

We sat there, the heater blowing on us as the wipers moved in squeaking time to the radio. And for far too long, neither of us spoke. Something about her told me Michelle wasn't someone who'd ever understood feeling uncomfortable. I'd imagined she'd grown up in the suburbs of Providence, or maybe right here in Northwood, a child of a respectable middle-class family, who never had trouble making friends. I'd imagined she hadn't been teased much in high school. No, she was probably one of those girls the football players hung out with, or maybe she was one of the artsy ones who was just too cool for the others. I'd imagined she never had to come out. Unlike me, Michelle was probably that girl who could say or do anything, and no one would dare tell her otherwise. Maybe that was why she smiled at me, a quiet, beguiling smile, her full, rosy lips pursed together, just begging to be kissed, while I squirmed in awkward silence.

"Well? Are we just going to sit here all night?" I'd known Michelle for just over four weeks, and already she was unlike anyone I'd ever met. No one had been able to get to me quite like this. No one could prod me, taunt me, take jabs at me that carried this enigmatic, crazy juxtaposition of bullying and infatuation. She was the little girl in kindergarten who pushed you off the monkey bars and then held your hand. And you loved her for it.

"Now I know you didn't drag my ass over here for that." She laughed and patted my knee.

"Look at you! Learning to give it right back to me."

"I can't imagine many people do."

"Not many at all. Do you want to know where you're taking me?"

"It might help if I'm driving." Michelle's hand still rested on my knee, the warmth of her skin penetrating my jeans.

"When was the last time you went to the museum?"

I put the car in reverse and backed out of her driveway. "The museum?"

"Yes. You know, that place with the art?" She gave my knee a small squeeze.

"It's been…God, I don't know. Years. Why?"

"Take a left here. Onto the highway." I did as I was told, flicking my blinker and merging into the light, late-evening traffic. "Stay on this for fifteen miles. Then take the exit for Providence."

My throat grew tight and I clenched the wheel.

"Providence? I can't—"

"Relax. It's an art museum. Not a porn convention." My tension eased a little, and I even managed a tentative smile her way. "They're open late on Saturday nights."

"But Beth—"

"Is at work, right?"

"Yes."

"And she doesn't get home until late, right?"

"Yes."

"And it's just an art museum, right?"

Wrong. It was anything but "just an art museum." Just a little road trip to the city. Just a late-night outing with this insanely beautiful, sexy, smart woman who wanted to take me on a cultural excursion. It was exciting and rejuvenating. It was everything I wanted in my own marriage but could no longer find.

"Yes." I couldn't tell her what was really on my mind.

"Good. I promise I'll have you home in time." I cringed a little. Back then, I'd thought I was rebelling against the confines of marriage. Things like curfews were for teenagers. Who was Beth to tell me when I had to be home? Oh, that's right. My wife. Back then, I'd assumed I was just being the jerk I'd always written myself off to be. As it would turn out, though, I just hadn't found much worth tying myself down for yet.

Chapter Four

It wasn't a long drive to Providence, and I secretly wished I could slow it down. Michelle's hand still kept its place on my knee, not moving any farther up but not moving away either. Every few minutes, she'd lean forward and fiddle with the dials on the radio until she was satisfied with whatever song came on—anything from Top 40 to jazz. Beth had a vanilla taste in music, limited only to whatever was on the iTunes best-seller list or the country album she'd been listening to since high school. I loved jazz. I grew up on jazz. When I was a kid, my grandfather used to take me to see this band, the Willy Howard Band, at his favorite bar. I was way too young for a bar, but I wasn't too young to appreciate the swinging melodies and pitchy trumpets. Of course, Michelle would love jazz too. Couldn't I find just one thing about her that wasn't stupidly enticing?

At her direction, I pulled into the lot at the museum, where a crowd of brave, artsy night owls in raincoats and black leather boots had gathered on the steps.

Michelle paid for my ticket, and I wasn't quite sure whether to feel emasculated or flattered. I was the lawyer. Beth was the bartender. And, although I made pennies at the firm, I still paid for everything. I always had. Not necessarily because

Beth expected it. Just because. Because, really, I got off on "wearing the pants." Beth had always made me feel strong, and powerful, and in control. She used to, at least. She stroked my ego like a kitten, never letting me forget just how much she needed me.

It wasn't that Beth didn't try to expose herself to the arts and culture and the ways of the world outside of Applebee's. It was that she only did it for me. She did it because it was important to me. I tried to make that mean something. But it just didn't. And eventually, she simply stopped caring.

"This one's my favorite," Michelle said, breaking through my rambling thoughts and pointing to a beautiful Masaccio of a man begging at the feet of another in a crowd of robes and head coverings. "Everyone likes Michelangelo," she went on, "but I think Masaccio was the real genius of the Italian Renaissance."

I stared at her, dumbfounded, my eyes locked into hers. She slid her arm through mine and smiled again, this time glancing at the floor, just for a fleeting instant reminding me of a shy, love-stricken teenager.

"I was an art-history minor in college," Michelle explained.

Nope. Not a single thing about her that wasn't stupidly enticing.

It was nearly eleven, and, aside from the lone security guard with the flashlight and a couple making out by the pottery exhibit, we had the place to ourselves. We weaved through the dark pathways, commenting on every piece we came across. Eventually, I ran out of original things to say, describing every work I saw as "bold," or "dramatic," or "avant garde." Fucked if I knew what I was talking about. Being a lawyer, though, seemed to give me all kinds of credibility I hadn't earned, including critiquing the Italian Renaissance.

When I first came out, back in high school, I'd dreamed of my perfect girl. She was sort of a composite of every strong-headed, killer-bodied woman I'd come across, sprinkled with a little bit of my neighbor who tutored me in biology and my mom's best friend, Susan. I'd always imagined this girl would take me to a museum, or a play, or a concert. And not a junky punk concert in the downstairs of Shooters either. As I got older, though, I'd discovered the reality of the shallow depth of the lesbian dating pool. And eventually, I'd given up on finding anyone who could check off half of the none-too-complex list I'd created. In my naive, entitled mind, even after striking off "must love the Red Sox," "must be a Scorpio," and "must be a middle child," everyone seemed to fall short.

I'd always wanted to find someone who could appreciate the world—someone who found value in other cultures, and travel, and exploring things that weren't part of the everyday. But that was a want I'd given up on long ago. Northwood was a small town. But even UCLA lacked its share of lesbians with any kind of substance. Besides, love isn't about getting everything you want in someone. It's about compromise. I guess what I didn't realize back then was that compromise and settling didn't have to be the same thing.

"You hungry?" I asked Michelle, with just the slightest hesitation, as we came to the end of the exhibit.

"Never been hungrier. Come on, I know just the place." Of course she did.

Before I could object, she'd grabbed my hand and pulled me back through the museum and out to the car. I went around to open the passenger side for her again. "You're really getting the hang of this chivalry thing." She crossed in front of me, until we were standing in the small space left by the open door, our faces so close I could smell the sweet peppermint on her breath. I'd never wanted to kiss anyone quite so much.

There she was, her perfect lips just inches from mine. It would have been the easiest thing in the world to lean forward, just a little bit, and silence the need that was all but eating me alive. Kissing her would have been easy. Restraint, that was the hard part.

Instead, I settled for watching her climb into the seat and gently closing the door after her.

Michelle led us to a quaint coffee shop down the street that she swore made the best salted-caramel brownies on the eastern seaboard.

"What about Beth?" she asked, carefully. "She doesn't do the whole art scene?"

I let out a skeptical chuckle. "No. It's not really her thing. She tries, I mean, or, she used to. For my sake. But we don't... We don't do things like this."

"So, what *do* you do, then?"

I contemplated the question for a while, trying to come up with an answer that sounded more interesting than "sit around rotting our brains out with television."

"We like to watch baseball. And go to the movies..." I struggled for more, trying to remember the things we used to do when we actually enjoyed each other.

"My uncle has season tickets for the Sox!"

"No way. You're a baseball fan too?" I matched her blistering excitement.

"Are you kidding? I was at game seven of the ALCS!"

"The Aaron Boone home run?!"

"Yes!"

"Horrible!"

"I know! I cried. I wish I could say I was joking, but I'm not. Cried like a baby the whole way home." She laughed at herself in the most adorably self-deprecating way possible.

Must love the Red Sox? Check.

"I would never have guessed you were a sports fan." I stuffed the last of the chocolate into my mouth.

"Don't be so quick to judge, Alex. Just because I have long hair and wear skirts doesn't mean..." *Damn. First foot-in-mouth moment of the evening.*

"I didn't mean that how it came out. I just meant...Well, you're beautiful is all." Before I could stop them, the words tumbled out of my head and straight to my mouth, which definitely still contained my foot.

"You think I'm beautiful?"

I couldn't quite tell if she was teasing me again or if I'd inadvertently managed to penetrate her near-constant state of cool.

"Of course I do. Have you ever met anyone who didn't?" Her eyes drifted down toward the table, and she was quiet for the first time all night. "What? What did I say?"

"Nothing. Really. It's fine."

No woman in the history of the world ever said those two words and meant it. But Michelle was willing to let it go for the moment, instead handing me a sad smile and taking a sip of her coffee. The world teaches you that monogamy means never finding another human being attractive for as long as you live. I tried that for a while. But I was sure even Beth looked at other women this way. Still, it didn't stop the guilt that flowed from saying the words aloud.

"What time does this place close anyway?" I asked, noticing the young kid from behind the counter sweeping the now-deserted dining area. The last thing I wanted was to wander in after Beth and attempt to explain where I'd been all night.

"Two, I think. Why?"

I frantically checked my watch. 1:45 am. "Shit. It's almost two now."

"We better get you home then."

We picked up the array of used napkins and chocolate-smeared plates and headed for the door.

❖

I didn't want the drive to end. Ever. Sometime after we'd crossed the Fillmore Bridge, Michelle had stopped talking, her head slowly and innocently drifting to my shoulder, where it landed. I carefully reached to turn the radio down, not caring anymore what the clock on the dash was telling me. Maybe I wanted Beth to find out I was with Michelle that night. I didn't know. What I did know, though, was that nothing had ever felt better than her soft, sleeping head against my cheek.

I slowly maneuvered the car into her driveway, dreading the moment I'd have to wake her up and leave her.

"Michelle." I turned, the fragrance of her hair that tickled my neck filling the air in front of me. She groaned sweetly, as if trying to push the grogginess away. "We're here." She lifted her head and flashed me a smile heavy with sleep.

"I can't believe I fell asleep. I'm so embarrassed."

"Oh, don't be. I didn't mind at all." I more than didn't mind. Those fifteen miles were the best I'd had in, well, in far longer than I cared to think about.

"I had a really good time tonight," Michelle said earnestly, going for her seat belt.

"Me too. I needed it. Thanks for dragging me out."

"Yeah, well, I hope I didn't have to do too much dragging." She laughed and went to reach for the door handle. "Good night, Alex."

And like that, she was gone.

It was 2:20 a.m., and Beth's truck wasn't parked on the street outside our apartment. A swell of relief came over me. I was in no mood to fight tonight. I changed into sweatpants and buried myself under the down comforter.

I didn't hear Beth make it home because I was fast asleep.

CHAPTER FIVE

Sunday morning came early, and I was up long before Beth was even awake enough to turn over in bed. I made my cup of coffee and sat on the living-room sofa, the B-list version of *Good Morning America* on in the background. Eleanor Cohen's Red Bull case lay open in front of me. My coffee dates, for lack of a better term, with Michelle had provided a new opportunity for me to really work on my career again.

I'd come out like a bullet at UCLA. Top twenty in my class. Volunteer for every internship or extracurricular. Superstar, future JD. But then, something happened. I graduated and started working at the firm as a paper-pusher. There were no jobs for new grads—even the best new grads. But I had hope. And a future. Mr. Watson, of Watson, Johnson and Smith, said I'd do great things there. He said he'd make sure of it.

And then came Beth. No, that wasn't fair. It wasn't her fault I'd spent the last three and a half years in a job that was on the fast track to the mailroom. I became complacent. And before I knew it, my misery at home had seeped into all other corners of my life, until I felt inexplicably hopeless, destined for a life of bickering and a wife that had become more like a roommate.

But coffee with Michelle seemed to be changing my

attitude, somehow. I told myself it was the extra time I was putting in on Saturdays while we sat at the café. The truth, though, was that it probably had more, much more really, to do with Michelle herself. Being around someone who was so passionate and driven by their work, by what they loved, was contagious. All of a sudden, I was on fire again, willing to do whatever it took to climb to the top.

My cell phone sat next to Eleanor's case file, taunting me with its silence until I was forced to pick it up and start to type in a text message.

I had a great time last...

Delete. Delete, delete, delete. Let her come to you. No! Don't let her come to you! Stay away. You're married. Stop it.

A war was raging in my head—one that confused my fingers, which were constantly typing and then deleting again until, exhausted, I threw my phone onto the couch beside me and buried it under a pillow.

❖

"You're late today," Michelle said. It was Tuesday, my second new favorite day of the week. After Saturday, that was. Saturdays weren't confined to lunch breaks or office hours. And, under the guise of work, which I sometimes actually did there, we could stay until the last coffee bean of the day was ground. Still, any day that led to Michelle was my favorite day.

She was sitting in her usual spot in the café, her blue scrubs on and a larger-than-life coffee in front of her.

"And just how long have you been obsessively waiting for me?" I came to her side, giving her my coyest smile. Her face flushed a crimson that made my insides turn over. She paused, thrown off only momentarily by my unusually suggestive tone, then looked at the clock. "Seventeen minutes."

"Not much fazes you, does it?"

"Not much at all."

I sat down on the stool next to her and started pulling apart the bagel she already had waiting for me. This was the best hour of my week, without question. Those sixty minutes that I'd spend on that stool, at that counter, eating my mostly stale bagel next to Michelle, talking about work, and life, and food, and family, and anything else that came up…those were what got me through the week. I went home at night to Beth fueled by the sparks that showered me whenever Michelle was around. I didn't know what got her through. I guess I didn't really want to know, either.

"How was your weekend?" Michelle asked, comfortably, like we'd been doing this for years. Like we'd continue to do this for years.

"Oh, it was okay. Pretty standard. Except for this nut job who kidnapped me and made me drive her to the art museum in Providence on Saturday."

"What?!" She feigned horror, raising a hand to her mouth. "The nerve of some people! She should be arrested."

"I don't think anyone would dare."

She gave me a quick wink and put her hand on the small of my back. "But really. I meant what I said the other night, Alex. I had a great time with you."

"Same. I can't remember the last time I—" I stopped myself. Lately, it felt like all I was doing was making a running comparison of Michelle and Beth. What foods they liked and disliked, what movies they hated, their laughs, their eyes, their jobs, their everything. It was sick. Like some twisted pro-and-con list you use to help make a difficult decision. These were people, not two vacation destinations. It was sick. Sick, and wholly unnecessary. After all, Michelle and I had shared nothing but a few cups of coffee and some Italian paintings— hardly the kind of activities that warranted a life-changing decision.

Girls like Michelle didn't stay single for long. She was beautiful, that was true. Stunning, even. But pretty girls were a dime a dozen. What made Michelle so irresistible, what made it so impossible to believe she could be sleeping alone, was her wit. Her charm and magnetism that left me hungry for the next thing she was about to say or do.

I had to laugh at my own ego. What kind of delusional world was I living in? Girls like Michelle Masters didn't go for girls like me. No. Girls like me? We ended up with girls like Beth.

"Well, anyway," Michelle said, politely filling in the silence I'd left, "I hope we can do it again sometime."

"So do I."

The big red clock on the wall in the shape of a hamburger taunted me. I hated 3:15 p.m.. Time to go back to the office. Time to leave Michelle. Time to wait four whole excruciating days until I could see her again. It was getting harder too, not easier. And the time between our coffee days was feeling longer and longer, until I found myself already daydreaming about another spontaneous phone call that would land me on another strange adventure with her.

"I have to get back," I told her, regretfully, picking up my leather bag and tossing it over my shoulder.

"Same time Saturday?"

"Wouldn't miss it."

The sincerity of my own words wracked my body with chills.

❖

I was a bullet again. George Watson, Jr., of Watson, Johnson and Smith, had taken notice of all the work I'd been doing on Eleanor Cohen's case and asked me to take the lead for the first time. It was small enough, sure, but I was putting everything I had into it. I went back to the office that day and stayed until nearly eight p.m., poring over data and trying to find out exactly how to take down the distribution company who failed to properly package their energy drinks that had led to the old lady's hip fracture.

The ringing of my cell phone jarred me out of my work-induced hypnosis. *Beth.* It had to be. I was late for dinner (as if we actually had a set time for meals and weren't eating cold chicken tenders), and she would be worried. Or jealous, or paranoid, or whatever she would be. But she would definitely be something. Beth was reactive. That was for sure. And I dreaded the grating, high-pitched octave her voice adopted when she was not-so-discreetly pissed at me. The name on my caller ID wasn't hers, though.

"Michelle?"

"So I need a favor. A big one."

My heart exploded like a bomb in my chest, nearly knocking the wind out of me. "A favor? From me?"

"Yes, genius. From you." *Anything. Anything you need.*

"Sure, shoot." I rocked anxiously back and forth in my chair.

"I need a plus one."

"Excuse me?" Silence.

"Ugh. Let me start over." I could hear how flustered she was even through the phone. "These friends from work are getting married on Saturday. And I can't bring myself to go alone."

I sat for a long time, trying to process exactly what she was asking of me. A date? To a wedding?

"I know what you're thinking. A date to a wedding is a lot of pressure. But I swear to God it's not. I just need some arm candy to get me through this thing. That's all. And the fact you're a friend makes it all the less painful."

My stomach sank. The three words no one wants to hear from a pretty girl—"You're a friend." Of course I was a friend. What would make me think I was more? I was still wearing that stupid ring on my finger that said I couldn't and wouldn't be more than that, anyway. Still, it would have been nice if she'd wanted more. I was admittedly enjoying the fantasy of a relationship not so devoid of passion and intensity—as if such a thing even existed. I wasn't entitled to feel so disappointed about nothing. But the selfish jerk of a few years back still liked to rear her jerky head now and then. "Such an enticing offer. You want me to be your escort." I laughed lightly, hoping it would cover some of my inexplicable sadness.

"Please? I'll beg if I have to."

"Go on—"

"Oh, you bastard. You're really going to make me work for this, aren't you?"

"Where's the fun in it for me if I don't?"

"I'll buy your coffee for a month. No. Two months. And all your bagels with that disgusting excuse for jam."

"Not good enough."

"Come on, Alex! There has to be something you want from me."

Something I want from you? Okay. I want to take you home, or better yet, I want you to take me home. And I want to undress you. And I want to kiss you for three days straight until you beg me to stop and then…Enough, Alex.

"There is this one thing—"

"I'm listening!" Her voice perked up eagerly.

"Remember the Eleanor Cohen case I've been working on?"

"You mean the very confidential Eleanor Cohen case?"

"Yes, that one. The partners just asked me to run point on it. It's going to be my first time going to trial, and I'm a little nervous."

"That's un-fucking-believable!"

I felt the heat rush my face and my lips form a shy smile.

"Thanks. If it goes well, I could make partner next year."

"I'm so proud of you! But wait…what do you need me for?"

I paused for a while, more than a little embarrassed to be asking what I was. Ridiculous, maybe. But I'd find any reason I could to get in a few hours with her. Even if it meant a little bit of humiliation on my end.

"I need you to dress me."

Michelle erupted with laughter, but I remained quiet.

"Oh my God. You're serious, aren't you? You're completely serious."

"Yes, I'm serious! And if I'm going to be your, what is it you called me? arm candy? for this wedding, you owe me big."

"Okay. Done. Anything you need."

"Meet me tomorrow at five thirty at the Nordstrom in Belmont," I told her.

"I'll see you then. I hope you're ready for this, Alex."

But I had no idea if I was.

CHAPTER SIX

Michelle was standing in front of her Toyota when I pulled into the damp Nordstrom parking lot that evening, holding a paper coffee cup and crudely pointing to the spot on her wrist where her watch would have been, had she worn one.

"Why do I have a feeling I'm about to regret this?" I said through my open window.

"How dare you!" I put my car in park and got out. "Come on. This will be fun. I swear." She threw her arms around my neck and my heart raced. I stood there in the parking lot, holding her waist as the light rain misted around us, thinking how long it had been since I'd known just how powerful one embrace could be. Beth and I hardly even hugged anymore. And it was amazing how good something so simple could feel. Without another word, she pulled away and led me into the store.

"How about this?" I said, picking up a blue-striped oxford off the rack.

Michelle frowned in disapproval.

"What?! What's wrong with it?"

"First of all," she yanked the shirt from my hands, "it's way too casual. You need something that says 'high-powered attorney.' This just says 'high-school dance.' And there's no way you're a men's medium." I raised my eyebrows at her. "See? I told you this would be fun!"

"So what then? You want to get me in some kind of femmie power suit?" That same creeping disappointment visited me again, and I wondered what kind of girl she usually went for. Maybe it wasn't the tie-wearing, pink-hating variety of dyke. Maybe Michelle was into other frilly sapphic princesses. Maybe her painful use of the f-word was less about my marital status and more about me. Speculation was pointless, anyway. I didn't need her affection. I had to keep reminding myself of that.

"Oh no. God, no. You'd make a horrible femme. You're way too handsome."

I was frozen in place, the heat rising from my belly up to my ears. I would undoubtedly spend the rest of the day replaying her words, looking for meaning where there might have been none. Meaning that, really, wasn't allowed to mean anything anyway.

"Well, good then." I was stuttering.

"This." Michelle rushed over to a rack in the corner that held a perfectly tailored charcoal-gray two-button suit. "This is what you need." She hurried back to me and thrust it into my arms. "And try this with it," she said excitedly, handing me a striped dress shirt.

I came out of the fitting room feeling like I looked almost good enough to be seen with her. The gushing smile on her face seemed to suggest the same.

"Yes. Yes, yes, yes." She stood and clasped her hands together, still smiling with her perfect, white teeth.

"I take it this meets your approval?"

"You look…" She paused awhile, seemingly ready to say something else. "It's perfect. You look like my not-quite-date to this wedding on Saturday. And one hell of an attorney." I beamed at her.

❖

Come Thursday, I still hadn't told Beth I was going to a wedding she wasn't invited to. And as Michelle's stand-in for a date too. I knew it was now or never, as I walked toward the front door that night. I'd seriously contemplated the "never" option too. But I'd already done enough lying around Michelle. And why should I have to lie? Michelle was a friend. We'd done nothing more than talk and run off for a couple of innocent field trips behind my wife's back. What could be so wrong with that? But I knew the wrong wasn't really in what we were doing. No. The wrong was in what I was feeling.

"Beth, I have to tell you something, and I don't want you to get mad." Well, this was off to a pretty great start. She defensively jerked her head away from the God-awful sitcom she was watching and turned it toward me. Beth always reminded me of a snake when she looked at me like that. Like she would strike, leeching venom into my veins at any moment.

"What did you do this time?"

It wasn't completely unfair of Beth not to trust me or to think I was a Class-A dickhead. When she met me, when I was so, so much younger, that was more or less what I was. I'd managed to cheat on every last girlfriend I'd had. When I was with one, I was flirting with another on the back burner, just waiting for the moment I got sick of the current one. In the spirit of full disclosure, I'll admit all that. Because that's nothing like who I am now.

Five or six years ago, my goal was to rack up so many notches on my bedpost it looked like a grad student's sad attempt at modern art. Beth knew all of it. Every last disgusting play I made. She was my best friend—the one I told everything to when we'd drive out to Adam's Point and just sit in the car watching the sun go down over the marsh. She knew everything, and she'd loved me in spite of it.

But the longer we were married, the more she seemed to be waiting for me to regress to those days. Her jealousy and snide comments were growing by the year, until the trust she'd once found in me was left buried in the naivety of youth.

"I didn't do anything! Christ. I just…I have this friend who wants me to go with her to a wedding this weekend. And I'm going to go." There. It was done.

Now I just had to wait for the bombs to go off. I just had to wait for the snake to launch her deadly teeth into my neck.

"A friend? Which friend?"

"A friend from the office." Okay, so maybe I wasn't *completely* done with lying.

"Which friend, Alex?" She scowled her snake scowl.

"You, uh, you don't know her. Her name is…Sarah. She's in…accounting." I gauged her face to see just how much of this story she was going to buy.

"And why does she need you to take her?" Beth asked, skeptically.

"Her husband's out of town, and she doesn't want to go alone. It's an old friend's wedding and she doesn't know anyone there." God, I was such an asshole. Why couldn't I just tell her it was Michelle?

"You're sure this woman is straight then?" *Oh, yes. That's why.*

"As an arrow. All she ever talks about is sex with this guy. Gross. I'm telling you. Straight as they get."

The pinched look on her face eased a little as she contemplated my request.

"Fine. Do what you want. I don't care." She truly didn't care. And I wasn't sure anymore why she insisted on continuing the charade.

"You're sure?"

"I told you it's fine. Just don't do anything stupid."

I walked out of the room fuming. The trust was gone. But I already knew that. What unsettled me through and through was the feeling that we'd both just stopped trying.

❖

I couldn't concentrate on Eleanor's case at all on Friday. The articles I read and phone calls I made went right through me, and all I could think about was the wedding—what Michelle would be wearing, if she'd want to dance with me. Damn it, I almost forgot about dancing. I couldn't dance. Not well, at least.

I remembered our wedding day, Beth's and mine. We were too poor to pay for a real venue, so instead we settled on a strip of beach and some picnic tables outside one of the town's hotels. While we sat, eating our budget fish dinners with our closest friends and family, one of the locals, known for his downtown performance pieces, lugged a boom box over to us and belted "It Had to Be You" in a scratchy baritone. The sun was pounding down on us, but we were too busy laughing and listening to our guests share stories of our childhood and our earlier days to notice.

A few lines into the ballad and my cousin started chanting, "Dance, dance, dance." So I took my new bride's hand and led her out to the sand that met the small outdoor dining area and held her. We swayed in a disorderly zigzag, laughing with only a hint of self-consciousness. But I don't think either of us minded when a crowd of pretty men in Speedos gathered around us and watched, some even taking it upon themselves to have their own dance. When the song ended, everyone cheered. And Beth had never looked more beautiful than with the late-afternoon summer light streaming onto her face and reflecting off her white dress.

I wished we could have held on to that feeling that day. But the memory was fleeting. Instead, I spent the day escaping into Michelle, imagining what she would say, what she'd do. And for a vulnerable second, I'd let myself imagine her long, soft fingers touching the back of my neck and her lips moving against mine. My stomach would flutter in a way it never had while thinking about something as simple as a kiss. Not even a kiss, a fantasy of a kiss. And then, I'd stop myself.

I'd made a promise. I'd changed. And I would never go down that road again.

❖

I stood in front of the long mirror in the bedroom, studying myself. My short black hair was parted to the side. My suit hit in all the right places, hugging my hips and my waist. A black silk tie was snugly in place around my neck. My shoes were polished and ready for any attempt at something I might try to call dancing. I was ready. And I'd never felt better.

Until I walked out of my bedroom and saw Michelle standing there. Then, I'd never felt better.

She leaned against the counter wearing a lilac dress that showed off her long, snowy legs. Her curls were done up on the top of her head, and shimmering diamonds hung from her ears.

"You look…" My jaw was fighting against gravity as I

tried to speak. She smiled shyly at me and did a quick spin, her dress twirling a little behind her.

"Thank you." She curtsied and then glanced nervously around the room. "So, is your wife home?"

"No. She's out with her sister for the night." Michelle relaxed a little and stepped closer, putting a friendly hand on my arm.

"You look pretty freakin' hot yourself, Alex."

My insides lit up and I bounced anxiously from one foot to another.

"I'm a fantastic stylist. If I may say so."

I laughed at her. "You certainly are. Should we go?"

"Absolutely." She took my arm as I led her out the door.

❖

The wedding hall was beautiful. The aisle was lit with white tea candles, and calla lilies adorned the front, where a ridiculously good-looking, short-haired woman in a black tux stood waiting. It was a small guest list. And it was readily apparent from the way they looked at the woman in the front that they knew her intimately.

"You didn't tell me this was a dyke wedding," I whispered to Michelle.

"Would it have mattered?"

"Yes! I'd have been much more excited."

She smiled, her eyes remaining focused toward the front, and gently smacked my arm.

I couldn't help but watch Michelle's face as the other woman, dressed in a gorgeous white dress, made her way down the aisle and took the short-haired one's hands in hers. Michelle's eyes were glued to the one in the tux, and as the two women exchanged their vows, a look that could only be described as old anguish came into them. I didn't know the cause. But it didn't take a genius to figure out there was history there.

"And do you, Charlie, take Natalie to be your wife?" the minister repeated.

"Are you kidding? Of course I do," the short-haired one known as Charlie said. Everyone in the crowd laughed and cheered. Everyone except Michelle. She extended the couple a cordial smile, but it was trapped behind a blanket of pain. As the two skipped back down the aisle, waving to their friends, I had to wonder what kind of moron would break Michelle's heart. Not me. No. If I had my life to do over again, I'd hang on to her with everything I had. Whatever, or whoever, it was that had hurt her so badly, I wanted to know. I wanted to fix it.

"You want to talk about it?" I prodded her gently once we'd reached our seats at the reception. The others at the table were up getting drinks and plates of food and mingling with the newlyweds.

"Talk about what?" But she hadn't smiled since the ceremony.

"How about what happened in there?"

"A wedding happened." Her usual teasing was missing some of its luster.

"Are you sure? Because you looked more like you were at a funeral." She was silent. "Look, you don't have to tell me if—"

"No. It's okay. It was a long time ago." I angled my chair toward hers.

"What happened, Michelle?"

She sighed from somewhere deep and buried. "I was in love with Charlie."

I looked at her expectantly. "I thought you were going to tell me what happened. That part was pretty clear."

"Well, aren't you insightful."

"Talk to me. No judgment, I swear. I'm your friend. And I want to listen."

She smiled and took my hands between hers, resting them on her lap. "Thanks. Really. I was stupidly in love with Charlie."

"Did you guys date?"

"I would hardly call it dating." She laughed painfully. "Back then, Charlie was a medic at Northwood. Natalie was the almighty doctor we all worshipped. And Charlie fell all over her the day she started there. Natalie was married, though, to this guy, nonetheless. Married with a young kid too. It was all really messy. They were hot and cold for over a year. And when they were cold, Charlie and I would get...involved." I squeezed her hands a little tighter. I wanted to break Charlie's teeth in for using Michelle to fill her time before Natalie came around. Michelle wasn't the girl you left when something better came along. She *was* that better thing.

"And?"

"And what do you mean, 'and'?" She laughed. "And we're here at their wedding. They're both great people. Great friends of mine, still. Natalie's the chief attending in the ED, and Charlie's the newest, and youngest, doctor we've got. They're this power couple. And they're totally, head over heels, worst-romance-movie-you've-ever-seen in love too." Michelle's eyes watered a little.

"And you hate them for it."

She giggled again, wiping away a stray tear from her chin. "Despise them." We laughed together as I instinctively took her in my arms and ran my fingers through her long, perfect hair.

"Stop that or you're going to smudge your eyeliner."

"Doesn't everyone cry at weddings?" she said defensively.

"Not because they're in love with one of the brides," I teased her, running my hand down her back.

"I'm not in love with Charlie anymore." She sat more upright and looked at me seriously now.

"Oh, I didn't mean—"

"It's not that I'm in love with Charlie. No. I gave up that ghost a long time ago. I've moved on. And she's one of my closest friends now. I'm not the same little girl who used to throw myself at her anymore." I winced at the image of Michelle kissing someone else—kissing someone else like I thought about her kissing me. "What bothers me is that…Oh my God, this sounds so lame. What bothers me is that I just can't help but feel like all the good ones are taken."

I touched her face with the back of my fingers. "Now that's just not true."

"Yes it is." She sniffled a little. "I mean, look at you."

"And what makes you think I'm one of the good ones?"

"Shut up and stop fishing for compliments." She was smiling again, her bold, beautiful smile that seemed to make everything else in the world okay. "Come on. Let's dance."

Before I could protest, she was on her feet, grabbing my hands and pulling me into her.

"Fine," I conceded, wrapping my arms around her waist, "but I warn you. I'm terrible."

Michelle wound her arms around my neck, resting her head against my shoulder. I could smell the musky perfume I'd always imagined she wore, as she fingered the short hair on the back of my head. "I don't know. You feel pretty good to me."

My heart beat in my throat. She lifted her head off my shoulder and locked her big hazel eyes onto mine. I felt myself moving toward her, slowly, uncontrollably, as if some force much bigger than myself was drawing us together. I felt my world as I knew it ready to collapse under the decision I was about to make. Or, maybe, under the decisions Beth and I had made together. The small space between our lips was hot and full of anticipation. I wanted to stop whatever was happening between us. I wanted to cling to my years of promises and my vows and my marriage, no matter how tangled it had become.

"There you are!" A voice cut through the silence that had fallen, the jarring sound breaking the electrified air around us and bringing reality sharply back into focus. Michelle pulled out of my arms and turned to greet the newly married couple standing in front of us.

"Hey, guys! Congratulations!" She hugged first Natalie, then Charlie, her eyes now vacant of the desire I knew I'd seen just moments ago.

"So glad you could make it," Natalie said.

"I wouldn't miss it."

"Aren't you going to introduce us to your date, Michelle?" Charlie asked. *Charlie. You asshole.* Without waiting for a reply, she extended her hand to me. "Hi. I'm Charlie. Thanks for coming today."

I returned her friendly smile and shook her hand, although I still fought the urge to introduce her face to my fist for what she'd done to Michelle. "I'm not really her date…I mean, we're friends. I mean, I'm Alex. It was a great wedding. Thank you so much for having me." As I pulled away, I caught Charlie's eyes wandering to the gold band on my left hand. She frowned and looked up at Michelle with questioning eyes.

"Well, anyway, we better let you two get back to it. Congratulations again, Dr. and Dr. Thompson," Michelle said enthusiastically.

"Oh, please. You really think Natalie would change her name?" Charlie took her new wife's hand and walked off.

Our wedding day had felt little like what I imagined these

two were feeling. This was a fairy tale—a real-life happily-ever-after. It was clear in the way they looked at each other, in the way they held each other, in the way they loved each other. I'd given up a long time ago on this kind of love, dismissing it as lesbian myth and deciding that living with your best friend was probably the next best thing to this nonexistent passion. But this was it. They had it. And I wanted it too.

"Are you all right?" I asked Michelle, once we'd sat back down at the table. Her coworkers and guests of the couple slowly joined us, but we were mostly oblivious. She was still visibly upset, her smile still missing that extra shine I knew she was capable of, although some of the pain seemed to have dissipated from her eyes.

"Yes. I really am."

I looked at her skeptically.

"I swear. I think I've officially closed the chapter on Charlie." She smiled at me and took my hand again. "Thanks, Alex. I'm really glad you came with me."

"Even if I'm a terrible dancer?"

"Even then. You're a great friend. The best."

We were great friends. That was all we could be. That was all we'd wanted to be. But that couldn't keep my stomach from falling to the floor like a brick.

❖

I wasn't at all surprised Beth had waited up for me. It wasn't terribly late, but I knew no matter what time it had been, she would have been waiting. She was curled up on the couch with a blanket watching *Real World* reruns.

"How was it?" she asked, clearly trying to hide the doubt in her voice.

"It was fine. You know how much I hate weddings."

"I know."

I took off my jacket and sat down beside her, kicking my feet up onto the coffee table.

My marriage to Beth had been a lot of things. It had been rocky and immature. We were scraping by on frozen pizzas and discount shampoo. Some days we couldn't even stand the sight of one another. But there had been a time, a time we'd both since forgotten, when we had felt love. Maybe it was never a fairy tale. Maybe we wouldn't get the ending Natalie and Charlie got. But I had loved her. I'd loved her as my best friend, who supported every crazy dream I had and every failure I endured. I'd loved her as the girl I came home to every night, who shared my bed and my cereal and my tubes of toothpaste. And she'd loved me.

I stared at the wall, trying to decide how long anyone could endure a relationship that had lost the things it was founded on, wondering if some kind of formula or flow chart existed that could help get us back to what seemed to be gone forever. But what I found was only cold, sterile silence.

"I'm going to bed," I said.

"Okay. I'll be in soon."

I stood in front of her, offering her my hands. "Why don't you come with me?"

Beth looked at me for a while, unsure of my invitation, until, finally, she returned my tentative smile and followed me to the bedroom.

I kissed her awkwardly, my hands fumbling with the tie on her sweatpants and the clasp of her bra. I couldn't remember when it had all stopped being so organic. She gave herself to me, her kisses and hands and embraces reflecting my hesitation, until we were both forcing fervor for the sake of fulfilling nothing more than an obligation. I wanted to feel it. I wanted to soar, even just a little, like we used to. I wanted to look at her like she was everything—like I could never love anyone else as long as I lived. But the feelings wouldn't come. Instead I used only mechanical, practiced gestures learned from years of making love to the same woman. Finally, Beth pulled away, sadness palpating the air.

"I'm really tired."

I reached to the floor and handed her the T-shirt I'd discarded. "Me too. Long day." We climbed into bed, a familiar three feet of space between us, and fell asleep.

Our bodies had been there. But our hearts? We had somehow left them behind.

CHAPTER SEVEN

I was trying. There could be little argument there. This was my life now. I'd made promises—life-long, forever kind of promises that shouldn't be taken back. After only a few years, I couldn't just up and walk away. I'd failed at every attempt at a relationship I'd taken, and I wasn't ready for my marriage to become one of those failures. I wasn't ready to face the world yet and say we'd made a mistake. We'd invested too much time, had too much love. I couldn't be the one to hurt Beth, no matter how bad things had become. And I couldn't break my own heart either. Maybe a miserable life with her was worth more than a lonely life without her.

I lay awake in the dark room, thinking about my parents. My mother went through husbands like she went through wine bottles, one after the other, always looking toward the next one. She'd nearly killed my father when she left. I would never be like her.

When we woke up the next morning, Beth decided she wanted to go to the casino. The one thing that hadn't changed over the years was her sense of adventure. I used to love the way she was always willing to pack up on a whim and go camping or take a road trip to some random city several hours away just for a hot dog. It was a haphazard kind of life that made everything new and exciting. Beth might not have been artsy, or educated, or culturally evolved. But you could never call her boring. Her impulsiveness had become tedious though. I didn't want to run off on childish adventures with her anymore. And it was rare she wanted to take me.

"You're shameless, you know that?" she said, as we walked through the penny slots.

"What are you talking about?"

"That girl." Beth nodded toward a blonde in a short blue dress sitting at the craps tables.

"What about her?"

"You just checked her out." She shot me an icy glare and pulled away.

"You're crazy. I did not." But I really didn't care what she thought about me and the girl with the blue dress. Beth was always accusing me of eyeing everyone, whether I did it or not.

"You don't really think a girl like that would go for you, do you?"

Wounded, I took a seat at one of the machines. "Why would I want her to, Beth?"

"Because. You want everyone to want you. You always have."

She knew how to cut me when she was hurting. She always did.

❖

I was trying. That was true. But that still didn't seem to keep me from counting down the days, hell, even the hours, until I could see Michelle again. Finally Tuesday came, and the waves rolling through my stomach as I walked to the café did little to disprove just how much of an effect this girl had on me. She was there, her hair up in a loose knot, looking tired from a long night at work, but more beautiful than I'd ever seen her. More beautiful than I'd ever seen anyone. I ached with a wanting I'd never known before. It was painful, and invigorating. And I wanted that moment back, at the wedding, where I held her with my arms, and she held me with her eyes, and I couldn't tell where my hold ended and hers began. That moment where we were so close, all the wind had to do was shift to bring our lips together. I quietly damned Charlie for stopping it, although I knew I should have been thanking her for saving my marriage— or whatever was left of it.

"Hi." Michelle stood when I walked in and hugged me.

"Hi, yourself." I hung on a little longer than I probably should have before we finally sat down.

We ate our sandwiches and caught up on the first parts of our week—the hospital, Eleanor Cohen and Mr. Watson, Michelle's cranky sister with the annoying Shih Tzu. But she shifted uncomfortably on her stool, seemingly distracted by everything around us.

"Are we ever going to talk about it?" she finally blurted out.

"What, exactly, are we supposed to be talking about?"

"Oh, I don't know. The Yankees series? The president's visit next week? Or, how about that near kiss at the wedding the other night? We could talk about that one."

I was stunned to silence. Was it a near kiss? I'd thought so. But, then again, I'd also managed to convince myself I'd completely romanticized the entire evening. Our entire friendship, actually. Not this time, though. That moment on the dance floor…That had happened exactly as I remembered it.

"Oh. That…" I said.

"Look, I get it. Weddings make me sappy too. We were

both vulnerable and maybe a little lonely. Let's just call it a wash."

A sharp pain rose in my chest.

"Right. A wash."

She looked at the wall behind me, avoiding my eyes.

"Thank God nothing actually happened." But she didn't look thankful.

"Yeah. Thank God for that."

❖

The summer snuck up on us, and before I knew it, it was June already. Charlie and Natalie's wedding that brought the near kiss had become nothing but a fond memory I often clung to at night while Beth slept next to me. Nothing even close had happened since. Michelle and I were picturesque best friends—taking walks in the sun, gossiping, getting coffee and wine. And every time she'd playfully sucker-punch my arm or talk about an ex-flame, I'd die a little inside, the air slowly being sucked out of my harmless infatuation.

"So where's the Mrs. today?" Michelle asked on one of our weekly walks through the small park in town.

"At the mall with her sister. They're shopping for our big Fourth of July party."

"And you didn't want to go?"

"You know you're the only shopping-buddy for me."

She smiled at me, the afternoon sun framing her face. I hated moments like those because she looked like something out of all of my dreams. Knowing she couldn't be mine hurt. And it shouldn't have.

"Glad to hear it. You guys are having a party on the Fourth?" she asked.

"Not us, no. Beth's parents." We stopped in front of a

tattered bench and sat. Michelle put her hand on my knee, and I put a friendly arm around her. She sank into me as the warm air engulfed us. And, like that, we were no longer just friends. We were two people who had loved each other tirelessly for decades, maybe longer. Two people who knew each other so thoroughly, even time couldn't weather them.

"Well, it sucks to be you then." Michelle stuck her tongue out at me like a child, and the moment was over, back to the sexless, eternal best friends. She might as well have been straight for all the interest she showed in me. The back-and-forth was confusing, and agonizing. But I couldn't fight the pleasure I felt when the platonic moments faded and I glimpsed a fantasy life I'd never be able to have.

"Trust me. I'm not looking forward to it. We do this every Fourth. Her parents have the whole family over. There are, like, fifteen kids running around the pool screaming. Her dad gets completely wasted, her mom cries, and her sister yells at them. Beth, of course, joins in the yelling. And I pretty much just count the hours until it's over."

"Sounds like my hell," she said.

"Mine too." We laughed a little as we watched two little boys kick a soccer ball with their father a few yards away.

"It's too bad you have plans already," Michelle said, turning toward me with a small grin.

"It is?" Something about the way she was looking at me made my pulse trip.

"Yeah. My aunt has a place in Provincetown. I'll be there for a few days, you know, if you wanted to come with me."

I stared at her in silence, gripped by images of lying on a strip of beach in P-town with Michelle, getting ice cream on Commercial Street, and watching the queens at the Crown. And I hated Beth. I hated being married.

"Well, I…"

"I know, you have to go with Beth. Obviously. I was just saying, it would have been fun." Michelle put her arm around me and ruffled the back of my hair.

"It would be really fun…I wish I could go. Another time this summer, maybe?"

"Maybe." She smiled. But we both knew that would never happen. We both knew there weren't enough excuses in the world to get away from Beth for a couple of days. She would lose her mind if I asked, no matter how innocent it would be. It just wasn't worth a fight.

"I should get home."

"Of course. Me too," Michelle said.

We reluctantly stood up and walked toward my waiting car.

❖

The dreaded Fourth of July blowout was getting closer, and every day I racked my brain for ways to get to the beach with Michelle for the weekend. I could tell Beth I had to work. But that might look a little funny when I didn't come home for three days. I could tell her I was visiting my family in New Hampshire. But she'd have a guaranteed aneurism when she found out I wasn't going to be spending it with *her* family. I could tell her the truth. But why? She didn't trust me anyway. There was just no way. I had to give it up and accept my fate—a truth that had become the story of my life lately.

"I have some really shitty news," Beth said, sitting down next to me on the couch one evening. She fiddled with her fork and stabbed angrily at her frozen lasagna. I looked at her, expectantly. "My boss is making me work this weekend."

"This weekend? This weekend is the Fourth," I said,

trying to hide any sign of excitement that might creep into my voice.

"I know. He said he doesn't have anyone else. And everyone else has these expensive trips booked. I don't really have a choice."

"Oh. Oh, that's too bad." I fought the itch to jump up and pump my fists.

"He is paying me double. But it sucks that I have to miss the family party. Mom knows, and she expects you'll still be there." Fist-pumping session over.

"But I'd feel so weird going without you."

"They're really looking forward to it. You should go."

I casually picked up an issue of *The New Yorker* I'd already read and pretended to look at it. "I was sort of invited to this work thing. Maybe I'll go to that now."

"Really? A work thing? What kind of work thing?" Beth eyed me suspiciously.

"A work retreat," I answered with surprising speed and believability. "Yeah. Mr. Watson and Mr. Johnson decided to organize this trip to Boston for everyone for the weekend. It's like, some sort of team-building crap or something." *Well, that came out better than I hoped.*

Beth considered my story for a moment, tapping her nails against the arm of the sofa. "How come you never mentioned it before now?"

"I don't know. I guess I forgot." I hated lying. Even if it was to protect both of us from the unnecessary blows this would come to. But more than anything, I hated that I had to lie about something as beautiful and downright harmless as what Michelle and I shared. She had become my best friend. I shouldn't have to hide that from my wife. But I did. There it was then—Beth was jealous and over-reactive, and I was a liar. Not exactly soul mates for life. "I think I better go to the retreat anyway. You know, move up the corporate ladder and all that."

"This sucks." Beth sulked.

"I know. It sucks hard."

"There's always next year," she said, as if she didn't really believe her own words.

"Don't worry about it."

"Well, have fun at your little retreat then." She made sure to emphasize the word *retreat*, as if I were incapable of ever telling the truth again. I was angry and tired of always being villainized, until I had to wonder what we were even trying for anymore.

I waited eagerly for Beth to go to work, still reeling from the frustration of the last few minutes. When she finally left, I picked up the phone.

"What are you doing right now?" I asked Michelle.

"I'm still at work."

"Park or hospital?"

"Park." She laughed a little. "I've been stuck working on this proposal all day. What's up?"

"Want to grab a beer?"

Michelle paused for a minute as I tapped my fingers eagerly on the end table.

"Love to. I'll be done here in a few minutes. Let's meet at Shooters in an hour."

"Perfect." I hung up, smiling.

CHAPTER EIGHT

An hour later I walked into Shooters, the town's seedy pool-bar that most of us frequented at least a couple of times a month. The place was kind of disgusting. It smelled like Bud Light had been spilled on the stained carpet, and the lighting was always so dark you could hardly see the cue ball. It was the kind of place you went to without any expectations. But it was comfortable, and more than that, it was just where everyone seemed to meet up.

I scanned the room for her, but all I saw were a few young townies in trucker caps drinking beer at the bar, and a couple of college girls in skimpy tank tops pretending to shoot pool. I took a seat at a nearby table, ordered two Blue Moons from the redheaded bartender with a nose ring, and watched for Michelle.

"Hi, handsome." She grinned as she took the last few steps toward me. I stood and put my arms around her, wondering how I'd managed to keep my attraction for her so far at bay. I supposed denial was a powerful thing.

"Hi there. I got you a Blue Moon. Extra orange."

She blushed a little. "Nothing gets past you, does it? Such a lawyer." She sat down.

"How was work?" I asked.

"Insane. I'm trying to put together this massive event next month. The caterer just backed out, and the venue wants more money, and it's just been…Oh, never mind. Just boring stuff."

I reached under the table and touched her hand. "It's not boring stuff. I asked, didn't I?"

"Everyone knows that when someone asks 'how was work?' they don't actually want to know," she said.

"I do."

She weaved her fingers through mine, rubbing the band on my left hand.

"You sounded like you wanted to talk about something when you called."

"How'd you know?"

"Just something in your voice. You aren't as enigmatic as you think, Alex."

I laughed at her. "Damn. I was really going for this whole mysterious and sexy thing."

"I'm not sure about the mysterious part…" She let go of my hand and ran her fingers up my thigh, resting them just inches from the crotch of my jeans. I swallowed hard, afraid to move, afraid to breathe. I knew she'd never take it further than this. But I also knew she loved to watch me squirm under the weight of her torturous flirtation. And I couldn't say I hated it either.

"I did want to talk about something," I said, finally able to speak again.

"What about?"

"That offer for this weekend…down in P-town…Does it still stand?"

She smiled a big, toothy smile. "You know it does."

"I'd like to take you up on it, then. If that's okay."

"Are you serious? But how?" Michelle said, gushing.

"Beth has to work. Which means no family party."

"And she's okay with you going with me?"

"What? Oh. Sure. Yeah, totally fine," I said, stuttering. If Michelle knew I was lying to Beth about my whereabouts that weekend, she'd never let me go.

"Alex! This is the best news ever!" She stood from her stool and wrapped her arms around me, nearly crushing me with excitement.

"I know!"

"How about we celebrate by me kicking your ass at pool?" She was teasing me.

"Not going to happen. I'm a pro."

"Do you have any idea how much time I've spent here?"

"We'll see."

She led me to the pool tables, her joy still apparent by her quick, jittery movement. I picked up the pool cues and dipped them in chalk, handing one to Michelle, who was stacking the balls into the rack.

"Let's put a friendly little wager on this game," she said. A satisfying crack broke the pyramid and scattered them across the table, sinking several.

"What do you have in mind?"

Michelle circled, pointing with the end of her cue as she tried to set up her next shot. "If you win, I'll give you a haircut."

"A haircut? Why do you think I need a haircut?" I asked, running my fingers self-consciously through the overgrown tufts on my head.

"Trust me, you do. And I happen to be a damn good hair stylist. I used to cut my cousins' hair all the time."

"Why does that not surprise me?" I thought about renegotiating my terms. But the grin that emerged on her face told me not to. A haircut meant more time with her. It meant her hands running through my hair, her face close to mine.

There was something almost intimate when I thought about it. Intimate, without being intimate. Everything Michelle did was thought-out and meticulous. And this was no different.

"And if I win…" She smacked the cue ball, knocking three stripes into the pocket, one after the other. She didn't look up. "You have to tell me what you actually told Beth you were doing this weekend."

I froze, clenching the pool cue so hard my fingers were turning the color of chalk.

"I—"

"I'm no dummy. You've told me about Beth's hot streak. There's no way she'd be okay with her wife taking off to the beach for the Fourth of July weekend with someone else."

"But Beth…" I was stuttering.

"Come on, Alex. Don't play with me. It's insulting. So, do we have a deal? I win, you tell me where she thinks you'll be when you're really with me."

I nodded silently as she went back to sinking the stripes.

Finally, she missed one. I lined up my shot, gently running the wood through my thumb and forefinger. I was terrible at pool. I'd played maybe twice in law school, and I'd been plastered both times. The white ball soared across the table, missing its target by about six inches and bouncing off one wall, and then the next, until it dropped in the corner pocket.

Michelle was focused, quiet, zeroing in on the lone stripe left in front of us. She hit the ball into a dizzying spin, where it nicked the green stripes, which drifted perfectly to the middle pocket.

"Right corner," she said, pointing her cue. Michelle angled the stick just right and smacked the eight ball smoothly into the hole. "So," she said, looking up from the game with a triumphant smile, "where are you going this weekend?"

I sighed, putting my cue on the table. "I'm going to a work retreat in Boston."

Michelle laughed and took a long sip of her beer. "A work retreat? Very clever." Her face dropped a little. "Look, I don't condone lying. But I also know how bat-shit crazy girls can be. We aren't doing anything wrong by hanging out on a beach for a few days and eating lobsters. So I won't harp on you too bad. But you should think about telling her the truth."

I nodded.

"So you really think I need a haircut, huh?" I asked.

She took a few steps toward me and pulled my hair through her fingers. "I do. Big-time. I know I won the bet, but I may just be feeling charitable enough to do it for you still."

"Is that right?"

"You better finish that beer and take me up on it now, though, before my charity runs out." She smiled.

"We can go to my place. Beth's at the bar."

"Sounds like a plan."

❖

"Do you even have scissors?" I asked Michelle once we'd settled into my apartment. She'd spread a garbage bag on the kitchen floor underneath one of the stools from the breakfast bar and began rummaging through the junk drawer under the sink.

"You must have scissors somewhere in this house."

"Well, yeah, we do, but don't you need some kind of special haircutting scissors or something?"

"Stop worrying so much. I'm going to make you look great." She whipped out a pair of industrial-grade scissors she found, and I eyed her warily. "Aha! Here we go!"

"We use those to cut the mats out of Jed's fur."

"So, I'll wash them! Just relax. I've got this."

Michelle disappeared into the bathroom while I put on some music and opened another beer. She reappeared holding a plastic spray bottle filled with water and a comb.

"Where did you find all that?" I asked.

"In your bathroom. Every girl has one of these." She held up the bottle. "You know, for those days you don't have time to wash your hair."

"Great. I'd offer you one of these," I pointed to my beer on the counter, "but I think I'll wait until after you're done with your hack job."

She laughed at me. "You think you're so tough. But you're loving this. You love attention."

"Excuse me?" I pretended to be hurt. "You think I love attention?"

"I absolutely do. You have two girls who're completely crazy about…" She blushed fiercely, regretting what had started to come out of her mouth.

"Crazy about what?" I wanted her to say it. I wanted her to admit what she felt for me had grown into more than the platonic undertones we'd been painting. But if she did, whatever it was would become real. And I wasn't ready for the consequences. I had to tread cautiously in moments like these, where Michelle was open and real. If I didn't, they'd shatter and disappear. These moments always did, eventually. I could only hope to hold them together for as long as I could.

"Never mind." There it went. I could almost see the tiny fragments of her vulnerability evaporate into the air. "Anyway, I'm ready to get started."

Michelle moved to my side and sprayed my hair down with cold water.

"God! You could have at least warmed it up for me."

"Are you always this difficult?" She squirted me one more time, this time intentionally hitting me in the face.

"Always."

For several minutes Michelle danced around me, bringing the scissors to my head and then pulling them away again, as if she were practicing. She scooped a patch of hair up in the comb and carefully snipped off what looked like several inches of my thick, black hair, which fell helplessly in a heap to the floor. I ground my teeth a little, trying to revel in the feeling of her hands on my head instead of the butchering that was surely happening in the meantime. This went on for a while, Michelle not speaking, not even breathing the entire time.

"Okay. I think we're done." She pulled the comb through once more and then used it as a level for the short bangs that were hanging on my forehead, gently and precisely parting them to the side, like I usually did, and rubbing a little bit of hair gel in. Her fingers on my scalp sent shivers down my entire body, and I involuntarily closed my eyes. "What do you think?"

She held up a small hand mirror in front of me, and I studied my reflection for a moment. She'd done a great job. None of my cowlicks were raging, and for once, I didn't look like I'd just rolled out of bed.

"Wow. Michelle, this is the best haircut I've ever had."

"You're just saying that."

"No! Honestly. You managed to make me look kind of… well, handsome," I said with a grin.

"You never needed much help with that." She brushed some hair off my shoulders, lingering just a little longer than necessary at the base of my neck. There were times, and they were usually small moments like these, where the electricity between us was so intense, it was blinding. It was as if the entire world burned up around us in the heat we'd created.

People always place too much stock in the big moments—the first kiss, sex, grand romantic gestures. But there's a lot to be said for something as small as a look or a brush of the fingers to the back of the neck during a haircut. Sometimes, less is way more.

❖

Friday was July third. The office closed early for the holiday, and I set off eagerly for home. Beth was there when I got in, surfing the Web on her laptop in front of MTV and a bag of Chex Mix.

"You're home early," she said, not bothering to get up from the couch.

"Everyone's going away for the weekend."

"Haircut?"

I pulled my hand awkwardly through my hair and looked just over her shoulder. "What? Oh. Yeah."

Beth closed her computer, staring me up and down for days. "Huh."

As much as I didn't want to care about something so minute and stupid, I did. Would it kill my wife to throw one tiny compliment my way? Too little, too late. For both of us. Still, I craved it. Almost as much as I was beginning to crave it from Michelle. Maybe Beth had been right when she said I wanted to be wanted.

"I have to get packed," I said, quietly.

"Oh, you mean the retreat in Boston?"

My face grew warm as guilt quickly displaced disappointment. "Yeah. The retreat. I better go. I have to leave soon."

I moved quickly into the bedroom, shutting the door to drown out the drivel Beth had playing on the TV. I opened my dresser and began pulling out shorts and tank tops and bathing suits, throwing them into my open suitcase. I couldn't get to Provincetown fast enough. It was going to be a little odd, admittedly, to be there without Beth. Especially considering that was where we got married. But nothing had been the same since then.

As I packed, the pits that had formed in my stomach as I looked Beth in the eye and lied to her began to heal. Something was happening. I wasn't sure if whatever it was was for the best. But I couldn't deny that it was exciting. I wondered what I'd be walking into. I could only assume Michelle's aunt and uncle would be there, or maybe some of those cousins whose hair she used to cut. What would they think of me? What would Michelle tell them? I had no idea what to expect. And it was all at once terrifying and thrilling.

I knocked on Michelle's door an hour later, after insisting to Beth that I'd be spending the weekend throwing back Scotches with a bunch of crusty old men and their bitter wives. I felt bad for lying to her. But then I'd remember the brisk silence that had settled between us and the quiet ways she'd cut me down whenever she could. I'd remember all the ways we continued to hurt each other, and some of the guilt ebbed.

"You all ready?" I asked Michelle.

"More than ready."

"Is this all you brought?" I picked up her enormous luggage that was bursting at the zippers, huffing dramatically.

"A girl has to be prepared for everything."

"You are so high maintenance."

"You love me."

But I wasn't even sure I knew what that meant anymore.

CHAPTER NINE

We headed east for three hours. The windows were down, blowing warm summer air in our faces as Michelle's favorite indie band blared on the radio. We sipped on iced coffee as I weaved in and out of the heavy Cape traffic. Every so often, I'd think of Beth, the frustration of failure creeping in. But then I'd turn to the passenger seat and look at the girl sitting next to me. At those moments, everything else would fall away. Michelle looked like a Kennedy in her oversized sunglasses and driving scarf that flapped in the wind—a modern-day Jackie O. She was everything that was elegant and beautiful. I'd have driven her to the ends of the world.

Provincetown sort of is the end of the world, actually. The town stretches no more than a couple of miles and revolves around one street, Commercial. When you stand at the end of the street, out near the Provincetown Inn, you're pretty much completely surrounded by water. Along with being one of the most popular gay tourist destinations, it's also one of the greatest little towns on earth. It pained me that I hadn't been back since the wedding. But the hotels during the popular months were expensive, and I hadn't really been set on a vacation with Beth anyway.

I drove up Bradford Street, bypassing the busy downtown foot traffic.

"This is the place," Michelle said. We turned off the weathered road into a driveway that led to a small cabin at the edge of the water. It was a soft yellow with blue shutters and a long wrap-around porch. A small dock extended into the receding tide.

"This is great."

"I'm going to warn you right now. Aunt Judy can get a little…pushy," she said.

"A relative of yours? Pushy? I can't imagine."

"Ha. Ha. But really. Don't be surprised if she asks a lot of questions."

"What kind of questions, exactly?" But before Michelle could answer, a tall, thin woman wearing Bermuda shorts and a blouse came running out of the house, her arms extended, ready to embrace somebody.

"Look what the cat dragged in!" The woman grabbed Michelle, who'd jumped from the car to greet her.

"Auntie Judy. You look fantastic." They hugged.

"You're such a bad liar. I'm turning into one of those old leathery beach ladies. But it sure is beautiful here, isn't it?" I stood behind Michelle, smiling uncomfortably and holding her ridiculously overpacked suitcase. "You must be Alex. It's so good to meet you. Michelle has told me everything."

Everything? What exactly did that entail? Auntie Judy extended her hand but then changed her mind and hugged me too, that kind of bouncing, giddy hug your mother gives you when you've been away for a while.

"Mrs. Masters, thank you so much for having me. This place is amazing."

"Thank you. We like it. Here, let me help you two with that. Michelle always did pack her entire bedroom." Judy picked up one of the smaller bags. "I hope you're hungry, Alex. I just made spaghetti carbonara."

"Starving. Michelle told me you were quite the chef. But she didn't tell me how young you were."

She smiled a proud smile and turned to Michelle. "You didn't tell me she was so charming, Shelley." Michelle blushed, and we followed her aunt into the house.

"We're just going to take this stuff upstairs, Auntie."

Michelle led me into a small bedroom with a double bed and two end tables, modestly decorated with a painting of a ship and a lamp filled with seashells.

Well, I guess this clears up the sleeping arrangements.

"She's great." I tossed my suitcase on the floor.

"Listen, there's something I have to tell you."

"What is it?"

She sat down on the bed. "Auntie Judy doesn't exactly know you're married."

"What do you mean she doesn't know I'm married? She knows you're gay, right?" I panicked, wondering what kind of conservative hell I'd just walked into.

"Of course she knows I'm gay. It's just that…well, she's been really hoping I'd meet a nice girl and—"

"And I'm that 'nice girl'?" I probably wasn't nearly as upset as I should have been.

"Sit with me." She patted the spot next to her, and I complied.

"So let me get this straight. Your aunt doesn't know I'm married. And she thinks we're dating?"

Michelle squirmed a little, then turned to face me with a pleadingly hopeful smile. "That's basically it. Please do this for me, Alex? Just for this weekend? She's been hounding me since things fell through with Charlie, and she really wants to see me happy. Ever since the cancer she doesn't have much to live for—"

"Jesus! She has cancer?!"

"No…I just thought that might add a little more weight to my plea."

"You're a horrible person, Michelle Masters." I loved to tease her.

"Let me just take a moment here to remind you which one of us has a wife who currently thinks she's trust-falling with a bunch of corporate baboons in Boston."

"Fuck. You're right. Okay, I'll do it. I'll be your girlfriend for the weekend. But only to save face."

Michelle just about tackled me, until I was pinned under her weight.

"Thank you, thank you, thank you!" She kissed my cheek, coming dangerously close to my lips, then pulled away, thinking better of it.

"And I don't want any funny business," I added.

She picked up a pillow and hit me in the chest, and we laughed, hard.

"Dinnertime, love birds," Auntie Judy shouted from downstairs.

"Showtime. Honey." I winked at Michelle.

She pointed to my wedding ring. "First, you better take that off."

"Oh. Yeah, I probably should." I twisted the band off my left hand and put it on the dresser, a distant sense of freedom washing over me.

❖

"So, Alex, Shelley told me you're a hotshot attorney in Rhode Island?" Judy asked.

"I'd hardly say that. But thank you. I just work for a sleazy little firm in Northwood. Mostly small stuff."

"Charming and modest," Judy said, gushing.

"Alex has this great case coming up. This cute little old lady slipped on a puddle of Red Bull in a Walmart, and Alex's firm is going up against this big distributing company. It's her first case on her own."

"You must be so proud of her."

"I couldn't be prouder."

I knew it was all make-believe. But it still felt so good to hear. I couldn't remember the last time Beth had been proud of me. Or anyone, really. I put my arm around Michelle and smiled, reveling in having someone by my side again who was happy to be with me, no matter the context.

"Tell me how you two met."

I froze with my pasta mid-twirl. Michelle looked at me, waiting.

"Go ahead, baby. Tell her."

"I…We…" I sucked in a deep breath. "Coffee…We met in a coffee shop."

"A coffee shop?"

"Yes. I was working on this distribution trial, actually. Michelle walked in and there were no other seats, so I told her she could sit with me."

"She insisted, actually," Michelle added. Judy was clearly engrossed, leaning on her hands and staring eagerly.

"Okay, I insisted." We laughed. "I couldn't help it." I looked at Michelle so long that everyone else at the table disappeared. It was just she and I. And everything that had been pretend momentarily vanished into reality. "She was the most beautiful woman I'd ever seen. I had to know her."

Michelle's eyes grew glassy and big, and she never took them off mine. She was good, I had to give her that. And for a fleeting minute, she'd almost convinced me too. Almost.

"That's so romantic," Judy said, breaking the spell between us. "Isn't it, Walt?"

Uncle Walter looked up, uninterested, from his plate of pasta and grumbled, "Oh yeah. Very nice."

"I'm just so happy Shelley finally found someone so wonderful. And handsome. You know, Alex, for me personally, other ladies just don't do it. But you are very attractive."

I turned a hot red. "I forgot to tell you about Auntie's candor," Michelle said, laughing.

"Thank you, Mrs. Masters."

"Don't call me that, honey. It makes me sound old. Call me Judy. No, call me Auntie Judy."

"Right. Auntie Judy." I smiled politely.

❖

I couldn't sleep that night. I never had trouble sleeping. Michelle lay quietly next to me, but all I could do was stare at the ceiling fan as it whirled over my head and think about what I was doing here. I'd called Beth after dinner and made up some story about flag football and burgers with the good ol' boys that sounded like something straight out of a Tommy Hilfiger ad. And then I went back to pretending I was Michelle's girlfriend, holding her hand and telling Auntie Judy how crazy I was about her.

I was happy pretending. I was happy having that fantasy, even if it was nothing more than an act. Beth didn't seem to care much what I was doing, anyway. She was quick to get off the phone with the excuse of the cat clawing at her feet, but I swore I heard someone else in the background.

"You okay?" Michelle asked softly. She rolled over and rubbed my back.

"Yeah. Can't sleep."

"You're thinking about Beth."

I turned to face her. "What? No. I'm not. Really."

"It's okay if you are."

"I'm not. I swear."

"Alex. It's okay. If you want to take off in the morning, I understand." She stroked up my arm tenderly.

"I'm not an awful person, Michelle." I felt heavy, wet tears invade my vision.

"Of course you aren't!"

My eyes gave way, no longer able to hold back the flood. "Things have just…they've really sucked lately…"

"It's okay. Really." She took me in her arms and wrapped me up in her, and I was instantly soothed. "You aren't a bad person. You're a wonderful person. The best person I know, actually. You aren't doing anything wrong. You've been completely loyal to Beth." But that somehow didn't feel like enough.

"I know. Thank you."

She kissed my forehead and held me tighter, and every worry I'd had vanished.

"I meant what I said. If you need to leave in the morning, I understand," she said.

"No. I don't want to leave. I want to stay here, with you."

A smile appeared on her face, even in the darkness. "Good."

"Besides. What would we tell Auntie Judy? I think she might be in love with me."

"You're gross." She laughed. "That's my aunt."

"I like the older ladies." I smiled and kissed her hand. "I think I need to call Beth."

"I think so too." Relief came like ice to a burn, and I felt like I could breathe for the first time in months.

"Good night, Alex."

"Good night, Shelley."

I fell asleep a second later, bathed in the sound of the lapping waves outside the open windows and the feeling of warm arms wrapped around me.

❖

"Wake up, you two. It's time for breakfast." Auntie Judy's voice came from startlingly close by, jolting me out of sleep. I squinted at her through the early morning sun beaming through the guest-room windows, grabbing the covers and shielding myself from view.

"We'll be right down," Michelle answered. "Just let us get dressed."

"Of course. How rude of me. I should knock next time. You'll have to excuse me, Alex. I forget sometimes that Shelley isn't a little girl anymore."

"It's uh…it's okay, Mrs…Auntie Judy."

"I'll see you guys downstairs," she said, and left the room.

"What the fuck was that?" I jumped out of bed and pulled on a sweatshirt.

"That was Auntie Judy, being Auntie Judy. She's… friendly."

I laughed. "She certainly is. What if we'd been naked?"

"Naked, huh? Now why we would do something like that?" Michelle reached over and ruffled the messy hair on top of my head.

"Well, you are my girlfriend, aren't you?" I said, playfully.

"Only when Auntie Judy's around."

"Hey, can't blame me for trying."

"I'd never dream of it."

❖

We sat down at the breakfast table, where Judy had prepared a feast of pancakes and waffles and chorizo and fritters and just about every thing else you could imagine.

"Can I get you some coffee…honey?" Michelle asked.

"That'd be great. Thanks…dear."

Michelle poured two hot cups of coffee and carried them over to me.

"So what are you two kids up to today?" Judy waited gleefully for our response, as if she was living vicariously through her niece's new "romance," while Uncle Walter sat, disinterested, reading the morning paper.

"I thought we'd take the boat out a little later, if you don't mind?"

"You know I never mind."

"You should come with us," I added.

"That's sweet, Alex. But I'm sure you two want some alone time." I swore I saw Auntie Judy wink at me from across the table. "Besides, Walt hates sailing, don't you, Walter?"

Uncle Walter looked up from the sports section and mumbled the first few words I'd heard him speak. "Too many sharks and things down there."

"There aren't any sharks." Auntie Judy cut into her pancakes with fierce determination.

"Are too. I saw this thing on Fox News the other night about great whites all up the Cape. Biting the legs off kids and everything. Won't see me swimming with those things. No way."

"Right, Uncle Walt, because we all know Fox is such a reliable news source."

Walt rolled his eyes up to his bushy eyebrows and went back to his paper.

"Anyway, I've got some great lobsters coming from Mac's if you two are planning to be here for dinner," Judy said.

I looked nervously at Michelle.

"Actually, I've already made reservations at Jimmy's Hideaway. I'm sorry. I can cancel them if you want."

"Don't be ridiculous." Auntie Judy waved her hand, dismissing us. "You have a romantic dinner together. Don't worry about us."

Michelle blushed. "Thanks. Well, we better get out there before the tide goes."

"You better! Have fun. Be safe. Don't go too far out. If you get into any trouble then…Oh never mind. You know what you're doing." Judy smiled at us, and Michelle stood to clear the table.

❖

"Is there anything you can't do?" I asked, tossing clothes aside in search of my bathing suit, once we were back up in the guest room.

"What do you mean?"

"I mean you're a nurse. You're an environmentalist. You're an art connoisseur. A wine enthusiast. A pool shark. And also a sailor?"

Michelle stopped brushing her hair in the mirror and turned to me, laughing. "I'm a Renaissance woman."

"You really are a Kennedy," I said, more to myself than her.

"How do you mean?"

I grinned at my not-so-internal monologue. "Never mind. But seriously. You know how to sail?"

"You better hope I do, since I'm taking you on the boat." She smiled playfully at me.

"You're amazing, Michelle."

"Have you called her yet?"

I felt my face fall. "I will when we get back. I promise."

"You don't need to promise me anything…I just think it's the right thing to do. What's the worst thing that could happen?"

I thought about it for a minute. "I come home to an empty house?"

Michelle picked up my cell phone off the dresser and threw it into my lap. "Would that really be the worst thing? Be the bigger person. I know you are."

She closed the door, leaving me alone in the room.

"Hi. How's Boston?" Beth asked when she finally answered.

"It's…Beth, I'm not in Boston."

An ominous silence fell over the line, and my heart thudded. I felt my life as I knew it about to crumble around me. And it was all at once frightening and thrilling.

"Where are you, then?"

"I'm in Provincetown." I tried my best to keep my voice level.

"What are you doing in Provincetown, Alex?"

"Just let me talk for a minute." I sucked in a deep breath. "I'm not on a work retreat. I lied to you. When you told me you couldn't go to your family's party, I knew I didn't want to go either. So I went to P-town with a friend—someone I've been hanging out with at the coffee shop once in a while. I should have told you the truth. I just didn't want you to get mad at me. I was a complete sissy. I'm sorry."

The silence grew until the only way I knew we were still connected was the slow, steady breathing on the other end.

"Are you cheating on me?"

"What? No! It's nothing like that. I swear to God. She's just a friend. The only reason I didn't say anything was because I know how jealous you get about other girls and—"

"We'll talk about this when you get home. I have to go."

My mouth hung open. "But I—"

"Have a good rest of your weekend, Alex." The phone let out three sad beeps, and she was gone.

CHAPTER TEN

We waded out to the small sailboat, moving in slow motion through waist-high water. It was only ten a.m., but the sun was already hot and the air was thick and wet. A dull breeze moved over the cool sea. It was a day exactly like my wedding. Michelle gracefully launched herself over the side of the boat and climbed in while I struggled to hang on to the metal ladder that swung off the back. I loved the ocean, but swimming and boating weren't my strongest suit. Michelle, on the other hand, had clearly been a fish out of water.

She went to work right away, unraveling the massive nautical ropes from the sails and cranking them open. "Here, hold this," she said, tossing me an end, while she tied a masterful knot into the anchor. Like everything she did, she made it look easy, natural. Faultless. It took everything I had to do anything but look on in awe. I watched her move through the boat, head covered in a sun-beaten Red Sox cap, her face set in a determined manner, thinking nothing would ever be the same again.

"Make yourself useful and open a couple of those sodas you packed, will you, Skipper?" She was teasing me. All I could do was smile helplessly at her and hand her a Diet Coke. With one hand she steered the boat skillfully through the harbor, weaving through moorings with a surgeon's precision while she took a sip from the bottle and smiled at me, holding my gaze for just a minute longer.

"How bad was it?" she finally asked, once we'd made it out to open water.

"It was...weird."

"Weird how?"

"Well, I honestly thought she'd divorce me for this one." I took a seat next to her.

"But she didn't."

"No. She was freakishly calm. I've never seen her act like that. It was almost as if...she didn't really care."

She smiled cordially at me, but something was missing. "I'm happy it went okay."

"Yeah, I am too." But I wasn't altogether sure I believed that. Coming clean to Beth had been two parts redemption and one part self-sabotage. Somewhere in me, a quiet voice hoped this would have been the end.

"How did you learn how to do this, anyway?" I asked.

"I spent every summer here with Auntie Judy and Uncle Walt after my mom left. It was my favorite place in the world. Still is, I guess. When I was ten, I started getting into trouble. A couple of the local kids took to me and convinced me to egg one of the neighbor's houses. Turns out he was this raging queen who made a big stink of it to my aunt, and she put me in this sailing club right away. She thought it would straighten me out. It probably did." She looked thoughtfully out to the blue-green water as she maneuvered the boat into the open ocean.

"They're pretty great, your aunt and uncle. And I'm sorry about your mom..."

"Don't be. I owe them everything. I'd probably be some

loser junkie like my mother if they hadn't taken me in. Or worse."

I took a couple of steps toward the helm and put my hands on her shoulders. "I think you did a lot of it on your own."

"And I think you give me way too much credit." The wind blew loose ends of her hair against my face and my neck, and I could smell her scent mixing with the salty ocean air. I closed my eyes and held her tighter, feeling her lean into me. "Here. You try." She slipped behind me, taking my hands and placing them on the helm.

"I don't know the first thing about driving a boat."

"You'll be fine. And don't call it 'driving.' You sound like a novice."

"I am a novice!"

She put her hands over mine and guided the wheel. "I've got you. I promise."

I steered the boat at a good ten knots, whatever that meant, actually managing not to sink us. And the smile on Michelle's face as I did made all the anxiety my effort caused well worth it.

"Looks like rain." She sent a worried glance to the sky. The sun had gone behind a large patch of dark clouds that seemed to come out of nowhere. We'd made it out of the harbor, and the strip of land that was Provincetown looked like nothing more than a distant blur from the deep sea.

"Is that bad?"

"It is if you don't want to get wet," she said with a smile. "There's some rain gear down below. Can you get it?"

The waves had picked up, rocking the boat back and forth uneasily and breaking against the bow. A loud, wailing alarm from above deck sent me scrambling up the steps, spilling the yellow raincoats as I went.

"Are you okay? What's going on?" I shouted. The sky was nearly black now.

"It's just the weather radio."

Weather alert for the lower Cape. Major storm system moving quickly out to sea. Swells at ten to twelve feet, winds at 40 miles an hour. The coast guard is advising all vessels to dock, or remain docked.

My head swam as I tried to keep the panic from showing. I loved being on the water. But I hadn't done it nearly enough to know what a problem might look like. This wasn't a problem. Was it? No. Michelle would tell me. This was just a little shower.

"Here," I said, tossing her the slicker just in time for heavy, cold rain to start falling.

"I need you to go below deck and make sure everything's secure. If anything's loose, tie it down."

I did as I was told, my anxiety building by the second. By the time I came back, the rain had soaked the seats and the deck. Michelle looked damp and worried, her hair in wet ringlets and her face stern. The sails flapped violently in the wind, and the boat tossed more and more with every passing wave.

"Is this normal?" My lips shivered in the sudden cold.

"Not really, no." She tried to look calm, but her knuckles where she held the wheel were as white as the angry, cresting water she was trying to fight through. "I think we're in trouble."

"What do we do?"

She didn't answer, just squinted into the horizon as the waves crashed around us, the water getting higher and higher. She picked up the radio in front of her.

"Provincetown Coast Guard, this is the *Hail Mary*. We're

in the middle of this storm here and need help. Over." She didn't bother to hide her fear anymore. Her voice shook as we heard nothing but static. "Provincetown Coast Guard, this is the *Hail Mary*. Do you copy? Over." More static.

The *Hail Mary*? How's that for fucking irony? And if I hadn't been two knots away from my death, I might have even laughed.

Finally a scratchy voice answered. "*Hail Mary*, what's your location? Over."

"We're at forty-two twenty north, seventy-six thirty-six west. Over."

"We've got you, *Hail Mary*. Stay put. Over."

Michelle hung up the radio and began pulling at the helm.

"What are you doing?" I yelled. The rain was pouring now, the wind ripping through the sails overhead.

"I'm getting us home!"

I rushed to her and took her by the shoulders. "Are you crazy? They're coming to get us!"

"I can't leave this boat. Everything good that's ever happened to me happened on this boat!"

A larger, gray ship with US COAST GUARD painted on it emerged from the ominous horizon.

"Not everything, Michelle," I shouted. "Not everything good that happened to you. We happened." She turned from her post and looked at me, appearing dumbfounded.

"What are you talking about?"

"I happened to you. And if that's half as good as you happening to me...then it's better than any boat."

She contemplated my request and finally smiled at me through the rain. "I don't want to die, Alex."

"Me either. So let's get on this coast-guard boat and get the hell out of here."

A deep voice on a megaphone boomed from the nearby

ship. "This is the US Coast Guard. We're sending a raft over to get you."

We waited, the rain so heavy we could hardly keep our eyes open. Michelle stood in front of me and leaned against me. I wrapped my arms around her and we swayed with the boat. I swear I heard her crying through the storm.

A tiny orange dinghy manned by a guardsman in diving gear pulled up to the sailboat's ladder.

"Get in." He waved his arms. I helped Michelle down first, although God knew she didn't need it, then followed her, until we were both seated in the safe rubber vessel. The diver took us to the ship in silence, as four other men pulled us up on board.

"What the hell were you two doing out there?" One of them handed me a wool blanket, which I promptly put over Michelle's shoulders.

"It was fine when we left…" she answered, shaking.

"Didn't you check the weather? What's the matter? You don't have Internet?"

"Hey!" I stepped protectively in front of her. "That's enough."

"You're damn lucky we were nearby. I've fished enough of you rich kids out of the water to—"

"I said that's enough!"

The grumpy guardsman huffed and walked away. We sat on a steel bench, under the covered cabin. The rain still pelted the glass so hard I found it hard to believe it wouldn't shatter. But in the safety of the monstrous coast-guard ship, the sea seemed tame and reasonable, leaving me feeling almost foolish for convincing Michelle to desert her family's pride and joy.

"I'm sorry," she finally said.

"You're sorry? For what? You couldn't have known." I crouched in front of her and rubbed her shoulders.

"I should have checked the weather."

"Don't listen to that asshole."

"He's right. I almost got us killed. And I lost the *Hail Mary*."

"Well, with a name like that…" I smiled at her, and she slowly smiled back, until she was laughing, then crying in my arms.

"Alex…I have to tell you something." I looked at her. "I know you're married. And I know things are complicated, but I want you to know how I feel. Even if you don't feel the same way. Even if nothing can ever come of it. I just have to tell you that—"

But just then a tall, thin woman in a USCG hat and jacket approached with two steaming paper cups.

"I'm Lieutenant James. I'm sorry for Captain Howard." She leaned in close and whispered. "He's a bit of a prick." We all laughed together. "This storm came out of nowhere. Even we didn't see it." She reached out and touched Michelle's arm.

"Thank you."

"We'll go back out tomorrow and look for your boat. I can't promise that she'll make it through, but she stands a good chance."

Michelle's face brightened a little. "I'd appreciate that."

The lieutenant offered a salute and walked away.

"It's going to be okay. I promise," I told Michelle, putting my arms around her again.

"I'm so glad you're here, Alex."

"Me too." I rubbed her back up and down, willing the warmth to enter her. "Me too."

❖

Auntie Judy was so happy we made it back in one piece, she didn't even seem to hear that the *Hail Mary* might not be so lucky. Uncle Walt, on the other hand, wasn't quite as pleased. After a begrudging "glad you're okay," he went into the other room to sulk in front of the TV for the rest of the day while Michelle and I warmed up in the house with hot tea and sandwiches.

I called Beth later that evening, but she never picked up.

We went to bed early that night, exhausted from our brush with death and an evening of trying to cheer up Uncle Walt with single malts and Reese's peanut butter cups. But the first thing in the morning, Lieutenant James and her surly captain showed up at the front door to tell us the *Hail Mary* had been found. And she was alive. They towed her in to the mooring a couple of hours later, and I swore I saw Uncle Walt kiss the bow when they did.

CHAPTER ELEVEN

Put this on," Michelle said, after pawing through my pile of clean clothes. She landed on a white V-neck T-shirt and white jeans I'd bought on a whim last summer.

"All white?"

"We're going to a white party. At Pied."

"Don't I get any say?" I asked, playfully.

"Sure you do. Alex, would you like to wear the white T-shirt, or maybe you'd like to wear the white T-shirt?"

I laughed at her. "You're such a princess."

"You wouldn't have me any other way. Besides, it'll be fun. I promise."

"Every time you promise something will be fun, we end up getting stared down by an Evangelical couple while we're shopping for suits in a department store. Or crying at a wedding, or capsizing a boat."

"That is not true!"

I shot her a skeptical look.

"Okay, so maybe it's a little true. But this really will be fun. We'll have some drinks, and we'll dance…"

Shit. I knew what "dance" meant. "Dance" meant Michelle grinding against me, torturing me with her ridiculous body I wanted to touch so badly. It had been hard enough sleeping next to her the last few nights, keeping the proximity reasonable, doing no more than some harmless cuddling. Now, I'd be expected to hold it together while she dragged her ass down me in some dark club full of other lesbians, some sixty miles away from Beth, who was no doubt so furious with me she could hardly speak.

"Sounds great. I'll go get dressed." But by the time I turned around, white T-shirt choice in hand, Michelle was already naked down to her matching, soft-pink bra and panties. I couldn't keep my mouth from dropping open.

"What? You shy all of a sudden?" She was teasing me yet again.

"You're ruthless."

"Can't friends change in front of each other?"

Yes, of course friends can. But friends also don't want to fuck each other either. Heat raced between my legs as I pushed away thoughts of throwing Michelle down onto the bed and taking off the last of her skimpy clothing with my teeth...

"Sure." I turned my back to her again and pulled off my undershirt, then my shorts, feeling her eyes on me the entire way down.

❖

The inside of Pied, the most popular lesbian bar in Provincetown, was full from wall to wall with women decked out in white. Beautiful women of every kind: short, tall, butch, femme, dark, light, old, young. But I had the most beautiful of all of them hanging off my arm as we walked in. Michelle reminded me of an angel, which, after the previous day's events, felt more than appropriate. She was wearing a tight white dress that ended a few inches above the knee and a pair of simple, white strappy sandals. Her shoulders were already kissed with the July sun from just the few days we'd been there. Everyone we passed while we pushed our way through the dance floor stopped and looked at her. And she was there with me.

"I'm going to go get us some drinks," I said over the bumping bass.

"Rum and Diet." She smiled at me and wiggled her hips to the music.

I couldn't have been gone for more than five minutes, but by the time I came back Michelle was being chatted up by a tall, muscled younger girl with short, slicked-back hair and an expensive-looking button-down. Her slimy smile said she thought she could take home anyone in the place. I hated girls like these. I hated them because that could have been me four years ago.

"Here you go, baby," I said, loudly, stepping possessively next to her and staring down the bratty baby butch.

"Thanks,"

"Alex." I stuck out my hand, but the girl in front of me just gave me a cool nod.

"Jax."

"Well, Jax, we're all set here, so if you want to take off…"

Jax glared at me with her chilly blue eyes and turned to go.

"What was that all about, Ms. Jealousy?" Michelle said, sounding triumphant.

"I don't have any idea what you mean."

"You, tough guy! 1955 called and wants their ideal boyfriend back."

"I guess I forgot to turn it off, now that we aren't around your aunt. Besides, that girl was a creep." I was glad it was dark in the club, because I was undeniably hot and probably red.

"I liked her." Michelle began to shuffle around me, moving

her body to the beat. "She was cute." I did my best to copy her, although my body didn't move the way hers did. I don't think anyone's body moved the way hers did.

"She was twelve."

"She was nice."

"Nice? Her name was Jax. With an 'x,' I bet. And I bet the nicest thing you'd hear from her is your name, which she'd undoubtedly get mixed up with the other thirty girls she banged this week."

"You're so jealous."

"I am so not. I just think you can do better."

She put her arms around my neck and her body against mine, brushing me with her breasts until I could feel her hard nipples even through my shirt. My breath grew short, and I could feel the heat coming off her. Before I had time to think about what I was doing, I'd grabbed her hips and pulled her into me until her heat was coming through the front of my jeans too.

"You mean, better like you?" she whispered into my ear. Bolts of lightning shot through me, gluing my feet to the floor. Michelle continued to dance against me, a tantalizing smile on her mouth. I was her pretend girlfriend for the weekend. I was on a pretend retreat in Boston with Watson, Johnson and Smith. Would it be so horrible to have one pretend kiss?

"No. Not like me. I didn't…that wasn't what I meant."

"Lucky for you," she pulled away and smirked at me, "I already got her number."

I rolled my eyes in disgust. "Great. Be sure to invite me to the wedding. I bet you and Jax, with an 'x,' will have a very long and happy life together."

"You're an ass."

"Better be nice to me. I'm your girlfriend."

We laughed, but not without a hint of pain behind it.

❖

It was late by the time we reached Auntie Judy's front door, and I was drunk. Drowning in shots of vodka at Pied while Michelle slid her hand into the back pockets of my jeans probably wasn't the smartest plan I'd ever had. But it kept the thoughts away. Thoughts of Beth, sitting at home alone with Jed watching *Golden Girls* reruns over a couple of Hot Pockets. Thoughts of Jax, and every girl like her I knew was out there, lurking, prowling, waiting for Michelle to let her guard down just once, so she could sweep in and charm her way into her pants. Thoughts of the way Michelle moved, and smelled, and probably kissed...

"Tired?" Michelle asked, playfully stumbling into my arms.

I was tired. I was exhausted. I couldn't remember the last time I'd stayed out drinking until two a.m. But fatigue lost out to the feeling of her hair in my fingers and her body pressed against mine. I'd spent my entire life thinking. That night, I just let myself feel.

"Not even a little."

"Good." She moved away and took my hand, pulling me toward the water. "Let's go make a fire."

"A fire?"

"Come on. I do it all the time." For a second, I wondered how many beach bonfires she'd built with other girls. But the moon overhead bounced off the water, framing Michelle's glassy eyes and wild smile, and I realized I didn't care about the past. And I certainly didn't care about the future. Everything I wanted, in that moment, was in front of me, gathering driftwood from the sand and humming to herself. Everything that mattered was right here.

"Are you going to help me? Or just stand there and stare at my ass all night?" I laughed nervously, pretending to search for some suitable kindling. "Here, we need more like this," she said, holding up a piece she'd just picked up.

"Right. I know."

"Hold on a minute." I froze, but she kept talking. "You don't know the first thing about building a fire, do you?"

"Busted."

She smiled at me, slowly first, then began laughing, until she was so overcome she'd dropped to her knees, tears glistening even in the dim light.

"Oh, come on. It's not that funny!" I said.

"Oh…It's hysterical." She continued her boisterous, wonderful laughter that seemed to numb my body more than any shot of liquor, until I was laughing too. "I thought you were from New Hampshire," she said, when she was finally able to speak again.

"I am!"

"And you never learned how to build a fire?"

"I grew up in the city! We were twenty miles from the woods." I sat on the ground beside her. "Just don't tell anyone. I wouldn't want to lose my butch card."

She held up three fingers, looking me in the eye. "Scout's honor. Now get up and let me show you how to get this thing started."

I stood nearby as Michelle tactfully positioned the kindling inside the fire pit and lit the driftwood until a roaring blaze was billowing smoke into the night.

"You realize what this means," she said, sternly.

"No. What?"

She took a step toward me, and then another, until her breasts, covered by nothing but the thin cotton of her dress, were once again brushing against me, taunting me, tempting me to take things just one step too far. Instead, I managed to stay as still as death, watching, waiting for her next move.

"It means I just topped you." She pushed my shoulder and ran off laughing, reminding me of a kid playing tag.

"Oh, I don't think so!" I chased her, stumbling gleefully through the sand and grabbing her around the hips until we both tumbled to the ground. Before I knew what I was doing, she was pinned underneath me, my hands gripping her wrists and my lips a breath away from hers.

"Alex Harris," she whispered, hoarsely, a wave of desire shaking in her voice. "I didn't know you had it in you."

I was still for a long time, savoring the feeling of my weight on hers. Fuck wrong and right. Fuck my life back home. Fuck thinking. "Trust me," I whispered back, my tongue barely grazing her earlobe. "When I top you, you'll know it."

Michelle didn't move, didn't blink. But her breath came faster, and I felt her heart vibrating against my chest. Time was frozen. There was no right. Just us. Just this.

"I'm uh…I'm going to go get a blanket. I'll be right back." And in a single, smooth move, she'd slipped out from under me and was running toward the house. I curled my knees to my chest, staring into the orange blaze in front of me, wanting to be relieved she'd broken the hold I'd seemed to have on her. But I wasn't. I wanted her. And that was the only thinking I could do. Michelle came back a few minutes later, blanket in hand and the usual clarity back in her eyes.

"What's going on in that anxious little head of yours?" She was teasing me now, tossing the blanket on the sand and spreading it out next to me.

"Nothing." I smiled at her. "For once, I'm not thinking about anything."

Michelle slowly moved closer to me, running her fingers through my hair and kissing my cheek. "I don't believe that for a second."

"What? It's true!"

"I bet you're thinking how gorgeous I am. And how much you wish you could kiss me right now." My mouth fell open, leaving me searching for words. "Al. I was kidding." She laughed a little and I forced myself to join her.

"But what if…" I said, tracing her jaw with my fingertips, "what if that is what I'm thinking?"

Now Michelle was the one stunned to silence, searching my face for a sign of our usual flirtatious jesting that always danced dangerously close to the truth. But this time, it was gone, my walls disabled and my defenses paralyzed. She caught my hand and pressed it against her face, and I felt the silk of her skin over my entire body. "Then I'd probably tell you that I'm probably thinking something along the same lines…"

I shifted my body closer to her, circling my legs around her and placing my other hand on her cheek. The lapping water moved dizzyingly in front of us, and every muscle in my stomach clenched. I moved my lips toward hers, creeping slowly, as if to give her every chance imaginable to stop me. But she didn't. Not until we were so close we were nearly touching.

"You're really taking your role seriously," she said, chuckling awkwardly and turning her face just enough to divert my mouth. My heart dropped into the sand.

"Well, you know, I was quite the thespian in high school." Rejection. That's exactly what this was. But maybe, just maybe, if I could play it off on the booze, I could still save myself.

"I absolutely see it."

"I was Tevye senior year, you know." She'd pulled just far enough away from me now to break contact.

"Tell me you had to sing 'Sunrise, Sunset.'"

"You bet your ass I did. And I was magnificent." I began belting out the words in a scratchy vibrato until any leftover tension had blown away with the nearby smoke.

"Now I see why you became a lawyer." We laughed a little harder. "Seriously, though, Al…Please don't try to kiss me again…" My heart skidded to a stop.

"I…uh…"

"Please…I don't think I can stop myself twice."

❖

The weekend was over, and it took everything in me to convince myself to pack up the car and get ready to leave. I'd had a taste of the life I'd always wanted. And I couldn't imagine ever going back. I'd thought about staying. Maybe I could convince Michelle to live in a cute little bungalow by the water. She could serve coffee at Joe's, and I could sell T-shirts at one of those crap places downtown. The idea was impractical, to say the least. But I'd thought about it.

"Good-bye, Auntie Judy. Thank you for everything." Michelle hugged her.

"You take care, Shelley. Be nice to this girl."

I was up next.

"Thank you so much. And I'm sorry we almost wrecked your boat."

She squeezed me tight. "You're welcome here anytime, dear." Then, she leaned in close—so close, Michelle couldn't hear her. "You be good to her," she whispered, sweetly.

I nodded, resolutely.

It was Monday evening, but the July sun was still high in

the sky as I drove us down the single road that led out of town. The dunes were golden and massive, like mini-mountains made completely out of sand.

"I have a confession," I said. Michelle looked at me. "I don't want to go home."

"Me either. So let's not."

"What do you want to do then? Rent a little bungalow by the water and work at Joe's?" I was kidding. Mostly. But she didn't have to know the mostly part.

"Might not be so bad…" She had a sadness in her voice.

"I could think of worse things."

"Probably more realistic things too. You hungry?"

I wasn't. Not even a little. But dinner would buy me another couple of hours with her.

"Starved."

"Good. Me too."

I pulled off Route 6 in Wellfleet, just a town over, at a typical Cape shack that served fried clams and ice cream to families making the long trek back to civilization. We sat at a picnic table and watched a couple of kids run in the grass under a big willow.

"You want kids?" I asked.

"Two." She didn't hesitate. "What about you? You think you and Beth will have kids someday?"

And, with that, the fantasy I'd lived for that long weekend came crashing violently to the ground.

"I don't know. I mean, I've always wanted them. But we haven't really talked about it."

"Well, I think you'd be a great mom."

I thought she'd be a great mom too. I thought she'd be the kind of mom I'd want to raise my children—my nameless, faceless children who'd always been raised by a nameless, faceless woman by my side. Even after Beth and I met, I always had a hard time thinking of her as maternal. She was still a baby herself, after all.

But with Michelle, I could see it. I could see all of it. I closed my eyes, picturing fall Saturdays at peewee soccer games and family vacations to the Cape. I pictured her tucking them in at night, while I read stories. I pictured a future. A future I was never going to have with Beth.

"What are you thinking about?" she asked.

"Oh, nothing."

"No, really. You just went somewhere else. I want to know where. I want to go with you."

"I don't think you do," I answered sadly. She reached over the table and took my hand, stroking it with her thumb.

"Tell me."

I sighed deeply, lost in the depths of the world we'd created that weekend. "I was just thinking about what my life would be like if I'd made better choices."

"Quit being vague. What kinds of choices?"

"Maybe I wouldn't have gotten married so young," I finally said.

"Do you regret it?"

"You asked me that already...Remember? In the café?"

"I remember," she said. "But I also remember you never answered me. At least not honestly. So? Do you?"

I took in another deep breath. "All the damn time."

She looked at me in surprise, as if she'd expected a blatant lie. But I wasn't going to lie anymore. No matter who the truth hurt.

"Why?"

"Geesh. Talk about your hard questions. Who are you, James Lipton?"

She laughed at me. "You don't have to answer if you don't want to."

"No. I'll tell you." I chewed on a french fry and thought hard about how much I wanted to tell her. "I regret it because she isn't the one."

"The one? How many cheesy rom-coms have you watched lately anyway? There is no 'one.' Relationships are hard. They take work. And either you do the work, or you don't. Most people just don't."

"I don't think that's true at all. What about love? You don't believe in love?"

"Of course I believe in love," she said, seeming defensive.

"Just not in 'the one.'"

"I think you can love lots of people, in lots of different ways. So no, I don't think there's just one single person out of seven billion you're meant to be with."

"I never took you for a cynic."

"I prefer realist," she said, taking a sip through her straw.

"You really don't believe there's anyone out there for you?"

"Honestly, Alex? No. I don't. At least not who I'm looking for."

My heart dropped to my feet. It was all pretend, this world we'd created. Just a vacation away from reality. And now, I had to figure out if I could ever go back.

❖

I pulled into Michelle's driveway sometime after sundown, choking on the life I was about to walk back into.

"I'll get your bag," I said, opening the back door and dragging out her suitcase.

"Thanks."

"Well...anyway, good night." I turned to go, eager to escape the lingering heartache that wouldn't let up.

"Alex, wait."

"Yeah?"

"Thank you."

I shrugged. "You're welcome. It was…it was really fun."

"Yeah, it was. Alex?"

"Yeah?"

She reached out and pulled me into her, holding me so tight I could hardly let out a breath. "I miss you already."

"Me too." Big, stinging tears filled my eyes, and I quickly buried them in her shoulder. I knew what she meant. I would miss sleeping next to her every night. I would miss the way she looked at me when she said "good morning," the way she slurped her cereal, the way she made me coffee, and the way she sang to the car radio. I would miss everything about this fake life we'd made. And I knew she would too.

CHAPTER TWELVE

W eeks passed, but I was still walking around feeling like something had died. I went back to work, back to my apartment, back to my marriage, trying to go on like nothing was different. But it was different. It was all different. I'd been happy, truly, perfectly happy, for the first time in my life. And to have that all taken from me was like being doused in ice water after a hot shower. I couldn't deny that I was miserable before, but now I was dying. Something had to give.

"Don't forget we're having dinner with my parents at five," Beth said.

Fuck. The last thing I wanted to do was play the good wife with my in-laws all night.

"I know." I looked up momentarily from my computer. "I'll be ready."

I was in the middle of composing a lengthy email to Mr. Watson about Eleanor Cohen's case when a chat window appeared.

> *TreeLovingRN83: Hey there, handsome. Want to grab a*
> *drink? I miss you.*
> *Harris_Alex: Can't. Going to the in-laws' for dinner.*
> *Blah. Miss you...*

"What are you doing anyway?" Beth asked.

"Huh? Just working. Why?"

"You just got this stupid smile on your face."

"Smile? I wasn't smiling." My cheeks burned.

"Yes, you were. Who are you talking to over there?" Beth moved to my side, trying to peek at the computer screen.

"No one. I'm not talking to anyone." I slammed the laptop shut. "You ready to go?"

She eyed me suspiciously. "What's wrong with you? You're acting weird."

"I am not. Let's just go, okay?"

❖

We sat in tattered lawn chairs with Beth's mother, Ruby, the end of summer hanging in the air around us. My father-in-law manned the grill, tossing patties in the air and occasionally managing to get them back on the grate. His apron was stained with mustard and domestic beer, and he wore white gym socks with sandals. My sister-in-law chased her kids around the yard while they squealed with that kind of childlike energy that never runs out.

I loved those kids, my nephews. I was the one who taught Tommy how to ride a bike three years ago. And Jake, the older of the two, still came over to spend the night every time he got pissed at his mom. Every time I thought about leaving Beth, I thought about leaving her family too. Nights like these, I was reminded that, for all their faults, they were kind, loving, wonderful people who'd made me one of them from the very beginning. And not being part of that felt almost impossible.

"Aunt Alex, can I come sleep over soon?" Jake ran to my side, tossing a football in my lap.

"Sure thing, buddy."

"When? Tonight?"

I smiled at him. "Probably not tonight. But soon. I promise." He bumped his fist against mine, grinning.

My father-in-law handed me a cheeseburger on a floppy paper plate.

"How's the corporate world, Alex?" he asked.

"Oh, you know. Boring. How about you? How's the landscaping business?"

"Nuts this time of year. I can hardly keep up. I keep trying to get Beth to come work for me again, but she says she doesn't want to get dirty anymore. I thought lesbians were supposed to like that kind of thing."

"Dad. Seriously?" Beth stuck out her tongue.

"What? What did I say?"

"You're so embarrassing."

"Oh, come on. Alex is family. She doesn't care what I say. Right, Al?"

I smiled and nodded politely at him. My phone vibrated in the pocket of my shorts, and I instinctively reached for it. It was Michelle.

I know you had to run. Hoping we can meet later. Can't stop thinking about you.

My heart lightened like it hadn't done all night, even surrounded by family that loved me.

I'll call later.

I thought about adding one of those stupid cartoon heart things that cell phones have these days, but before I could, Beth grabbed it out of my hand and jumped away.

"What are you doing?" I shouted, far more aggressively than I intended.

"Who are you talking to? I knew you were a cheating shitbag. You always were!"

She was drunk already, furiously scrolling through my phone with her familiar venomous jealousy. But before she could get much further, Ruby stole it away from her, leaving her with nothing more than a furious scowl.

"That's enough, Beth. She's allowed to talk to other people." Ruby handed me back the phone, and I collapsed back into the chair feeling like I'd just dodged a Texas-sized bullet.

"What are you hiding? It's that girl you went away with, isn't it? That Michelle skank. I knew I shouldn't have let you off so easy. You're a fucking creep, Alex." Beth's words were slurred and messy.

"I think it's time for you to go upstairs and lay down," Ruby said for me.

Beth gave one last glare and allowed her mother to help her into the house and upstairs to her parents' room.

"I don't know what's going on with you two," Ruby said once she'd returned, "but I hope you can work it out."

I breathed deeply. And in that moment, I thought there was no working it out. There was no fixing what was never there to begin with. "I'll stay with her tonight. She should sleep it off."

"No. You go on home. She'll be fine here. I'll drive her back in the morning."

"Thanks."

I didn't really want to stay at my in-laws', anyway, waiting for Beth to wake up with a massive hangover and chew me a new one for what had happened. I still didn't know how much she'd seen before Ruby got the phone back. Whatever it had been, I wasn't looking forward to dealing with the repercussions in the morning.

I drove home alone, furious at her for not trusting me and furious at myself for giving her a reason not to. She'd been right to suspect. But she was far from innocent. Besides, I kept telling myself, I hadn't done anything more than tell a few harmless white lies. Worse than the lies, though, had been the sheer hatred that had flourished between us—hatred where love used to be.

I wanted to leave. I wanted to pack my things and never turn back, escaping the life of cruelty and bitterness we'd created. But I couldn't. No matter the harm she'd caused me, I couldn't hurt her. Not when she'd loved me. Not when I'd loved her. I wasn't strong. And leaving was just too hard.

I should have gone home. That was my plan, at least. But my car seemed to have a plan all of its own, as it almost involuntarily veered away from the turn-off for our street and straight down the road toward Michelle's. I needed someone who didn't have a thing to do with Beth or our lives together. I needed a friend.

"Alex..." She was wearing a stunning red dress, her eyes sparkling from the reflection of the moon overhead.

"I'm sorry I didn't call first. I just had a really bad night, and I needed to see you."

Someone appeared behind her—a taller, younger girl who I couldn't quite make out in the dark apartment lit only with a few candles. I could hear music playing in the background. Coltrane.

"I really wish you had." Michelle looked behind her anxiously, her usual warmth replaced by an almost unfamiliarity.

"What's going on?"

The tall girl stepped forward, out of the shadows, until she was standing behind Michelle, her hands protectively on her shoulders.

"Alex, right?" she asked. That pompous grin. That greasy hair. Those way-too-defined arms. I knew this girl.

"Alex, you remember Jax. Right? From Pied?"

My stomach lurched and my body begged to tackle her to the ground and slap that shit-eating smirk from her face.

"Yeah, I remember. Michelle, can I talk to you?"

She turned to Jax and gave her ridiculous bicep a squeeze. "Just for a minute, okay?"

"Sure." Jax shrugged, blankly.

"You're on a date," I said, once Jax was back inside.

"I mean, it's not really a date…"

"Did you fuck her?"

Michelle took a step back. "Excuse me?"

"Did you fuck her?" I repeated, slower this time.

"I don't see how that's any of your goddamn business."

I opened my mouth to speak, anger flowing through me like hot lava. But then I realized she was right. It wasn't any of my business. I was no one to her.

"I'm sorry. You're right." I sighed and sat down on her front step.

"What are you doing here anyway? I thought you were with Beth." She sat down beside me.

"I was. Until she got blinding drunk and blew up at me for your text."

"Fuck…I'm so sorry, Al…" She put her hand on my back.

"Don't be. I'm the one who should be sorry. I'm an asshole."

"You aren't an asshole. I promise you, no matter what you think you—"

"The thing is, though," I turned to her, "I'm not sorry. I'm not even a little bit sorry. For years now we've been pretending everything's okay, Beth and me. But it's not. It's not okay at all. We're...we're mean to each other, Michelle. We're fucking terrible. So no, I'm not fucking sorry."

"You don't really mean that," she whispered.

"I do. More than I've ever meant anything." I stood up, now towering over her. "But now you're on a date with Arms McGee in there, so I better leave you to it."

Michelle was silent as I started to walk off, my heart sliced to pieces.

"Alex." I turned. "It doesn't have to be that way."

But I wasn't sure I'd know what any other way would look like.

❖

I fell asleep alone that night, with the aid of a few tumblers of Johnnie Walker Red Label and Mr. David Letterman. Except I wasn't really alone. I had Jed, who was curled up on my legs purring wildly, and the irreconcilable sense that my life was slowly crumbling in my hands. My wife was passed out in her parents' bed, probably unconsciously cursing my very existence. Michelle was in the steroid-fed arms of a younger, better-looking girl, who was probably knocking her socks off in the sack. And I was alone.

"I'm sorry, baby." I felt Beth crawl into bed with me early the next morning, kissing my face and my ears and my neck. "I'm so sorry."

I mumbled incoherently, still trying to place who was next to me.

"Why are you sorry?"

"I shouldn't have taken your phone. I trust you, I swear I do." She kissed me again, resting her head on my chest. "I know you wouldn't do anything shady."

"Right…Well, thanks."

"You didn't do anything shady, did you?"

I sat upright, pushing her head away. "What? I told you I didn't!"

"I don't know how I'm supposed to buy that. You did lie to me and run off to P-Town with some whore." Her tone stiffened.

"I thought you said you trusted me! And don't call her a whore."

"I call it like I see it, Alex. All I can say is you better watch your step." She turned her back to me and curled on her side. "I have a massive hangover. I have to go back to bed before I barf."

I fought my own nausea that began to tumble inside of me. "Fine. Good idea." I jumped out of bed, put on some jeans and a sweater, and was gone.

❖

I didn't really know I was going to the café until I was about halfway there. We hadn't been in months. But something told me to go anyway. Maybe Michelle found herself there for the same reason.

She was sitting alone, at the counter, her Saturday glasses on and Salinger in front of her.

"Is this seat taken?"

She smiled. "You're so cheesy."

I pulled out the stool next to her and ordered a black coffee.

"So. I'm a complete jackass."

Michelle looked at me for a long time and finally erupted in laughter.

"Okay, so you're a little bit of a jackass."

"Forgive me?" I gave her the saddest doe eyes I could muster.

"How could I ever not forgive you?" She smiled and rubbed the back of my head. "How's Beth this morning?" She took a sip of her tea.

"Hungover. Sleeping. Just like any other twenty-five-year-old who works in the food industry on a Sunday morning."

"Is she mad?"

"It came to some blows this morning."

"I'm sorry, Alex…I really hope you can fix it."

I sighed loudly. "How about you? How was your date with Arms?"

She laughed, her cheeks flushing a little. "Her name is Jax. And she does have nice arms, doesn't she?"

"They're all right." I pulled up the sleeve of my T-shirt and squeezed my muscles as hard as I could. "Not as good as these though."

"Whatever helps you sleep at night," she said, punching me lightly in the shoulder.

"Are you going out with her again?"

"Why do you want to know?"

I fumbled through my head for a good reason, but nothing came to me. "I…Just wondering."

"Jealous."

"No way."

"Way. And yes, I probably am going out with her again." Her grin was mischievous and knowing. She was loving this.

"Well…good then."

"Yeah. Good."

"Great."

"Fine."

"I really am sorry. I didn't mean to just show up there last night and act like you were my…well, you get it." I turned away.

"Hey." She touched my shoulder. "I told you, it's okay."

I turned back to her, pushing a stray piece of hair from her face. "That weekend on the Cape…when we were…well, I just want you to know, I meant it…It wasn't all pretend…I mean…"

"I meant it too." She took my hand and gently pulled it away. "But it has to be pretend."

"I know." The pain and the need were crushing. "I should get home. Beth's probably ready for round two."

"You better. Bye, Alex…"

"Good-bye, Michelle."

CHAPTER THIRTEEN

It was Eleanor Cohen's big day in court. Or, really, it was my big day in court. I anxiously shuffled in alongside George Watson, Jr. himself, wearing the gray suit that made it difficult not to think about Michelle.

"Go get 'em, kid. You'll be great." Mr. Watson clapped me on the shoulder like I was one of his five sons, and I made my way to the front.

"Ladies and gentleman of the jury..." I said. My palms were wet, and my mouth was dry. This was my big chance— my only chance, actually.

In three hours, it was all over. The jury had unanimously found Brockton Distributors guilty of misconduct and unsafe food preparation in the case of Cohen vs. Brockton Distributors. Little Eleanor Cohen would receive fifty thousand dollars to cover her fractured hip, and another five for her pain and suffering. Of course, it didn't hurt that Mrs. Cohen was about four feet tall and reminded everyone of their grandmother. We had won. I had won. And I was elated.

George Watson, Jr., of Watson, Johnson and Smith, was smiling at me, his massive jowls swinging in full force as he made his way to the front of the courtroom.

"Well done, Harris. Well done." This time, he skipped the

manly clap on the shoulder and hugged me, emphasizing it with a firm slap on the back.

"Thank you, sir."

"By this time next year, I have a feeling we'll be seeing Watson, Johnson, Smith and Harris…" He paused a minute. "Well, not literally. The sign is already printed. But you get the idea."

"Yes, sir. That's great news."

"Take the rest of the day off, Harris. You've earned it with this one."

I reached out to shake Mr. Watson's hand one more time, and then he turned and left the courtroom.

I wanted to run out the door and tell everyone I met on the street that I was a real, live lawyer and not just a coffee-getter or envelope-licker anymore. I'd done it. I couldn't wait to tell…Michelle?

She was waiting in the lobby, wearing a light trench coat and slick heels. Her eyes looked like emeralds next to a green silk scarf that still revealed just a trail of skin leading to the opening of her blouse. She said nothing but instead began with a slow, steady clap and the proudest smile I'd ever seen on anyone.

"What brings you in here?" I just had to tease her. "I thought your days in a courtroom were finished after juvie."

"Hey, they let me off on good behavior." She moved slowly toward me, her face turning from jesting to a hazy desire.

"Good behavior? Unlikely."

"I can be very good when I want to be." She was standing so close to me now I could feel the heat radiating off her skin. She sucked in her bottom lip as she stared at me, holding me with those eyes that I felt completely helpless under. "I saw you in there."

"You saw?"

"All of it. You know they let just about anyone into these things? Because I didn't."

"Public hearings. I had no idea you were…"

"Back row, the entire time," she whispered. "You were amazing, Alex. So strong, and confident, and smart and…"

I looked at her expectantly as she stalled. "Go on?"

"And a complete misogynistic egomaniac."

"Misogynistic?" I scoffed. "Can women even be misogynists?"

"I don't know! But it was…safer…than what I was about to say."

I didn't ask, content with the knowledge that she wanted to say so much more than what she had.

"Come on."

"Where?"

"I'm taking you out."

I knew arguing with her would be futile. It always was. Besides, I couldn't deny the excitement that was bubbling inside of me at the sight of her. What was the point of even trying?

"And why would I want to do that?" I said playfully.

"Because I'm wearing a new dress under this coat, and I want to show it off. And you're officially a real, honest-to-God lawyer. A lawyer who just won her first big case. I won't take no."

"Well, I…" I thought about Beth.

"I won't take no. Besides, I heard that wrinkly boss of yours give you the rest of the day off. You have no excuses left."

Beth would be leaving for the bar right after dinner. She'd never notice if I wasn't home before then. Not that we'd been doing much talking lately anyway. Our late-summer blowout at my in-laws' had been the match that seemed to slowly burn away whatever had been left of us. Eventually, the jabs about my friendship with Michelle had stopped, and it was clear we were both just running on fumes. We were locked in a stalemate, neither of us daring to move, both of us irreconcilably miserable.

"Let me get my coat."

I grabbed my topcoat Michelle had picked out for me on our trip to Nordstrom earlier that spring. It was hard to believe summer was almost over, already. With the exception of a painful weekend in Boston with friends, Beth and I had managed to get by without killing each other. I was working more than I ever had to get ready for the trial, and we operated on basically opposite schedules that I was pretty sure kept us married. When we were together, we bickered, and argued, and rarely touched each other. But it was more than that. The things that used to be enough to keep us together—the security and comfort of knowing somebody would love you unconditionally—gradually didn't feel like enough anymore.

When I was with Beth, I felt stuck. And not just stuck in my marriage. I felt stuck in everything I ever was. I would be thirty soon, and when I was home, with my wife, I still felt twenty-four. Maybe it was her dead-end, college-student job, or my lack of income, or the crappy apartment we still lived in. Maybe it was the fighting. But one thing was obvious; with Beth, I was going nowhere. And it was getting harder and harder to remain resigned to my post as infallible wife.

"Are you going to tell me where we're going? Or is this another one of your infamous surprises?" I asked as we walked down the streets of downtown Providence near the courthouse.

"You love my surprises."

I answered her with a smile, gently putting my hand on the small of her back. I was always finding reasons to touch

Michelle. Even if it was something as simple as brushing a stray hair away from her face. I was starving for her. And if she'd made even the slightest attempt to take it beyond the platonic, I would have found it nearly impossible to resist. I would, of course. I had to. But fortunately, she hadn't tested that resolve. Michelle was above being somebody's mistress. She deserved more than that. And I was certainly not about to make her such. We had been involved in nothing more than months of excruciating flirtation, leaving me eternally emotionally and physically blue-balled. But I couldn't call it horrible.

"We're here." Michelle pointed to a small stairway that led to a dimly lit, stone entryway. There was no sign on the door, just an old iron knocker.

"Where is here, exactly?"

"When are you going to shut up and just learn to trust me?"

"I'm a lawyer. I trust no one."

She put her arm through mine in the way that always made my heart jump. "Isn't it supposed to be the other way around?"

"No. I'm extremely trustworthy." I pushed the heavy door open and held it while she went through.

"I know."

The unmarked door turned out to lead to the tiniest Italian restaurant in the city, with only five tables and the best veal Parmesan outside of Italy.

"How did you ever find this place?" I pulled her chair out for her.

"One of my many secrets. Red or white wine?"

"Red. What other secrets?"

"If I told you, they wouldn't be secrets." Michelle flagged down the lone waiter in a sauce-stained apron, who poured two tall glasses of an expensive merlot I never would have ordered otherwise. She raised it high in the air. "To Rhode Island's greatest new attorney."

We exchanged smiles and tapped our glasses. "And to a woman of many talents. One of which was picking out this dashing outfit."

"You did look pretty good up there..." Our eyes met.

"I'm more than just a pretty face, you know." I took a long sip of my wine, the dreamy fog building around me.

"You certainly are."

"So, how's everything with Arms?" I felt my eyes roll up into my head with jealousy.

"Things with Jax are...Well, they aren't."

I'd be lying if I said my heart hadn't suddenly grown wings and figured out how to fly in that moment. "Oh no. What happened?"

"She was just...not what I was looking for."

"Michelle, I'm so sorry."

She laughed at me. "You are not. You hated Jax."

"I didn't hate her, exactly."

"You hated her. And as it turns out, you were right. She was a total creep. I found out she was sleeping with half of Boston's dyke scene. Good thing I'm a lady and didn't give it all up on the first few dates. Go ahead, you can say it. I told you so."

Relief accompanied a deep sadness at the thought of her pain. "I'm sorry she hurt you."

"She didn't hurt me. In order for her to hurt me, I'd have had to have actually liked her. The truth was, as much as I wanted to be into her, I just wasn't. I sure did like how jealous she made you though."

"I was never jealous." Who was I kidding? She'd had my number all day long.

After a bottle and a half of merlot, we stumbled out of the

Italian hole-in-the-wall and onto the street. It was dark already, but the rain had stopped. The city skyline was lit up in front of us, the remnants of the end of a business day. As we made our way down Main, going where, I wasn't sure, Michelle brushed my hand with her warm fingers, and I couldn't remember the last time anything in my life had felt quite so perfect. And for what would undoubtedly be a fleeting moment, everything was simple.

"Nightcap?" she asked, casually.

"I don't know…" But I wanted to scream "yes" as loud as I possibly could.

"Oh, come on. It's not even seven yet. Unless Beth—"

"Where at?" I answered as if my stomach wasn't tumbling around in my chest.

"How about my place?"

My heart exploded, and my knees threatened to give out under the weight of every single fantasy I'd ever had about this moment. For so many months now, Michelle and I had met under the careful guise of being public. She hadn't allowed me to see more than the outside of her apartment, and I wasn't usually too eager to invite her to have cold Chinese food in the living room with Beth. I didn't trust myself alone with her. Not since our weekend on the Cape. Not when there were soft beds and lights that could be turned off and no one to walk in on us. I suppose Michelle felt the same. But at the end of the day, we all have choices. I just had to make the right ones for once. And as long as I was still married—as long as I still couldn't bring myself to hurt the person I'd sworn my life to—I would.

"Yeah. That works." I shrugged.

We took a cab back to Northwood, her fingers gently holding mine as the world raced by in a haze outside the window. I tried to convince myself I could stop whatever was about to happen.

"Right here," Michelle told the driver, and the cab stopped at the sweet yellow two-family I'd been outside of so many times before. She handed him a twenty and opened the door, not letting go of my hand until the last second.

I followed her through a dimly lit hallway littered by pairs of sneakers and rain boots, feeling like I was walking toward my fate, whatever that meant.

"This is it," she said, flicking on the kitchen light and hanging her coat on a chair.

"It's great." It was small, but the walls were painted a warm gold, and the furniture was worn and lived in, looking like it had been well loved for a hundred years. Some prints of the ocean and old architectural sketches were framed and hung in the living room. My place was so clearly furnished with my parents' leftovers, and the only things hanging were a photo of Fenway Park and my UCLA diploma. Everything in Michelle's home was intentional, down to the last lamp and refrigerator magnet. I felt like I'd opened up another piece of her just by being inside.

"It's not much. But it's home."

"It's you."

She extended me a bashful smile and turned to the cabinet above the sink, taking out another bottle of what looked to be a nice pinot noir. I knew if I had one more glass, any decision I made would not be grounded in rational thought.

I took the wine she poured for me anyway.

"Go ahead and have a seat in the living room," she said. "I'm going to go change. These tights are killing me."

Michelle disappeared into what I could only guess was her bedroom, as I collapsed onto a worn green sofa in the living room.

I was flipping through an old issue of *Vogue* when she came out again, dressed in a sheer cotton tank top with lace trim and a pair of loose sweatpants that fell just low enough to show the smooth skin on her lower back when she turned around. I wiped my palms on my pants as they began to sweat. There was plenty of room on the large couch, but she sat down so close to me one leg was nearly in my lap.

"Better." She smiled. "I hope it's okay. It gets really hot in here. Even this time of year." She chewed on her bottom lip a little and twisted a piece of loose hair around her finger.

"Yeah…" I swallowed hard. "It is a little warm." I slid my arms out of my suit jacket and tossed it onto a nearby chair.

"Here." Michelle slowly, painfully, moved her hands to the buttons of my shirt and unfastened just one, making sure to brush my neck with her nails as she did. "That will help."

But, of course, it didn't. The heat was worse than ever. My face felt like I'd spent a week straight in the desert sun, and my tongue was sandpaper against my mouth. I kept my hands, which were nearly as warm, hidden in my pockets, trying desperately to keep them from wandering.

And just as quickly as she'd been there, she was gone again, jumping up to put on some music. Jazz.

"Coltrane. My favorite," I managed to say, once I'd finally cooled down a little.

"I know. I remember." She sat beside me again, this time allowing for a little bit more distance between us—distance I fought to want to close.

My anxieties seemed to ebb with the second glass of wine, and inhibition was nothing more than an unpleasant memory.

"You're something. You know that, don't you?" I slurred my words drowsily.

"And what something might that be?" Michelle leaned up against the arm of the couch and swung her legs over mine.

"Don't take advantage of this inebriated state you've gotten me in."

"That was my plan all along." Her eyes were getting heavy.

"You're an evil genius."

"So what else am I?" She moved closer to me again, until her body was lined up with mine.

"Pushy. A little nuts…" I ran my fingers up the outline of her jaw and through her hair until her face was in my hand. "But also brilliant. And sophisticated. And sexy…"

She looked away, smiling.

"You think you're pretty charming, don't you?" she said to the floor.

"And cute."

She lightly pinched my arm and then grew oddly serious.

"You're trouble, Alex Harris. That's what you are."

The aching need in her voice was more palpable than ever. I felt any sense of control slip through my fingers and drift away.

CHAPTER FOURTEEN

I had no idea what time it was when I woke up. My neck was stiff and my head pounded, and it took several seconds to make sense of the soft body curled up against me. Michelle's face was buried in my chest, and my arms were holding her like I was afraid something would pull us apart at any moment. She was sound asleep.

Through the space in the blinds I could see nothing but black, and the only light on came from over the stove in the nearby kitchen. I slid out from under her as gently as I could and stood to check myself over. My clothes were all still on. My shirt was unbuttoned in several more places than it had been at dinner, but that didn't necessarily mean anything. Everything seemed intact, marriage included. But I couldn't remember a thing.

"Relax. Nothing happened." Michelle's soft voice behind me startled me to a jump.

"What? Oh, yeah, of course not. I remember."

She laughed a little.

"I was going to wake you up but…"

"No, don't worry about it. I didn't mean to fall asleep. I'm sorry."

"Really. Don't worry about it."

I looked at my watch, squinting in the dark room. Two am. "I better go."

"Yeah, it's late." But I swore I saw her face fall a little. I grabbed my jacket and we walked toward the front door.

"I had fun. Thanks for dinner. For everything, I mean." Nothing I could say seemed to mirror my intense spiral of emotions as I stood in front of her. I wasn't that girl anymore, the girl who threw out hearts like the week's garbage because she was on to the next best thing. Michelle was better than the next best thing. She deserved to be someone's last big thing. But I couldn't deny the piece of me that was raw with regret—regret for not kissing her, regret for not telling her I thought about her every single second of every single day, regret for not telling her I'd begun dreaming of walking out of my life as I knew it and maybe into a life with her.

Still, that kind of regret was tolerable. And I wasn't sure if uprooting my entire world was.

I was disgusted with myself for even considering walking away. Maybe I hadn't physically crossed any lines with Michelle, but I'd certainly crossed every other line available. I didn't know if Michelle felt something too. It didn't matter. This was the ultimate betrayal. I'd married Beth. I'd picked Beth. And regardless of whatever else had changed since, that had meant something to me. That had meant everything to me. I had stood in front of everyone I knew and promised to love, in some semblance of the word, my wife, for the rest of my life. Leaving would mean failure.

❖

I couldn't stop thinking about Michelle. No matter what I did or where I went, it wasn't enough to distract me from the memories of falling asleep with her. It hadn't been the first time.

We'd spent every night together on the Cape that summer. But this was different. This was in her home, on her terms. This wasn't about playing house for Auntie Judy. This was about wants, and needs, and feelings that even I couldn't fully guess the depths of yet. It was dinnertime, and I should have been going home to Beth. But I kept going, almost automatically, past our street and toward Michelle's.

"What are you doing right now?" I asked, once I'd dialed her number.

"Eating leftover noodles and watching Oprah. Why?"

"Want company?"

I could hear her voice light up through the phone. "I do if it's you."

"I'll be there in five."

A few minutes later, I was smiling again, pulling up to Michelle's.

"This is a nice surprise," she said, opening the door for me. I put my arms around her waist like I was seeing her for the first time in years, holding her tight and praying I'd never have to let go.

"I just wanted to see you."

"What's gotten into you? Come on, let's go in the other room."

I followed her to the living room, feeling like something of a lost puppy who'd just found its owner. I didn't know what had gotten into me, only that I was tired. I was tired of trying to be happy with Beth. I was tired of pretending I was happy without Michelle.

"I'm sorry about the other night." I sat down on the sofa, letting my head fall into my hands.

"Sorry? What could you possibly be sorry for?"

"For getting wasted and falling asleep with you."

"Please! If anyone should apologize it's me. I'm the one

who whisked you away for a romantic celebratory dinner and fed you wine all night when you should have been home with your wife. I'm the one who should be sorry, Alex." She put a warm hand on my back.

"I just hope I didn't do anything—"

"You were a perfect gentleman."

I looked up at her, her eyes as green as the ocean water that summer, big and hopeful and full of possibility. "I didn't even try to get to third?"

She smiled her smile that made my stomach flip and my heart pound. "Not even to second."

"What a loser."

"You aren't a loser," she said, seriously. "You're married. And I think you should try to work things out with Beth."

"I'm unhappy, Michelle. And normally I don't mind that part so much. But I'm not making her happy anymore either. I don't know what else is left to do."

"You just aren't trying hard enough. That's all."

Sadness and anger threatened to strangle me. "I should go," I said.

"I think so too."

❖

Beth and I sat in bed on Saturday morning, the TV doing its usual job of keeping conversation to a minimum.

"I want to meet her."

"Huh? Meet who?" I chewed on my cereal, thinking about what little ways I could temporarily escape my life that day.

"The girl you've been messing around with."

My blood heated. "I haven't been messing around with anyone, Beth. Are you done accusing me yet? I don't know what the hell else you want from me."

"I want to meet her. I want to see what kind of tramp has her hooks in you."

"You can't be serious." I turned to face her, looking at her for the first time all morning.

"As a fucking heart attack."

"You aren't meeting Michelle. She's just a friend. And if you can't trust me, that's your problem."

"Do you want to make this work or not, Alex?"

I was silent for a long time, my hard edge finally softening. "Do you?"

She sighed and fell back onto the pillow. "Yes. I do. We're married. This isn't just some throw-away relationship. I took those vows seriously."

"Yeah. Me too."

"Then prove it. If you want to stay with me, let me meet her."

"Fine." But I still wasn't sure what I wanted.

❖

"I'm going to the café," I told Beth, the following Saturday. I moved quickly for the door, hoping I could make it through without the question I knew was coming.

"Is Michelle going to be there?" Damn, she was fast.

"I don't know." Of course she was. "Why?"

"I'm going with you. I want to meet her."

"I…" My hand was on the knob, ready to help me escape. But I couldn't come up with a reasonable excuse to offer her. "Sure."

I thought about some kind of warning message—an SOS text message or secret phone call to alert Michelle to Beth's intrusion. But it was too late for that. Beth was tailgating me like a secret-service member, seemingly ready to bust me for whatever it was I was doing. Fortunately for me, I didn't think you could really catch someone's feelings. Besides, it was growing more difficult to continue caring what she thought.

We drove to the café, after I decided that a couple's bike ride might come across as a little too cutesie. The last thing I wanted to do was give Michelle the impression Beth and I were the happily married lesbian poster-children.

I walked in ahead of Beth, desperately searching for Michelle. She spotted me and stood, greeting me with her usual, boisterous smile. I watched as her eyes trailed behind me, her face falling, only for a second at the sight of Beth. And then, as if nothing were out of place, she was smiling again, this time more exuberantly than ever.

"Alex, you dickhead, she's gorgeous..." Beth mumbled through gritted teeth. Why was everyone always calling me a dickhead anyway? It wasn't like I'd asked for any of this. It wasn't like I'd told God how to make Michelle's numbingly tempting mouth or her smooth, white skin. It wasn't my fault she was perfect. To Beth, though, it would be.

"This must be the famous Beth Harris," Michelle chirped in a surprisingly convincing melody. *Add actor to her growing list of talents.*

"And you must be Michelle." Beth held out her hand, but Michelle ignored it and hugged her instead—the cordial, familiar hug your grandmother's friend gives you when she hasn't seen you in a decade. But Beth stayed cold and stiff.

"Alex has told me so much about you," Michelle lied. *Christ, someone give this girl an Emmy already.*

"So you guys do this a lot then." Beth wasn't asking.

Michelle and I exchanged tense glances.

"Oh, not that often. No, just sometimes. Once in a while. You know, when we both happen to be here."

"Right. When we both happen to be here," I reiterated.

Beth's eyes moved back and forth between us appraisingly. "Right."

"But Alex didn't tell me you were coming today. I'm so happy I finally get to meet you. She talks about you nonstop." *Bitches, she means. Bitches about you nonstop.* "Here, sit down, you two."

Beth took a seat hesitantly, eyeing the untouched bagel and full, hot coffee in front of Michelle. "Two coffees, huh?"

Michelle reached forward and pushed them to the side, continuing to smile at Beth. "Oh, yeah. They brought me two by accident. This place is always screwing up everything." She let out an anxious laugh.

"So, Michelle, Alex has hardly told me anything about you," she said, a hint of venom in her voice. Michelle looked wounded. Point, Beth.

"I'm not surprised. She's so busy with the firm and the big trial she just had, and this case that's coming up with the pharmaceutical giant is going to be—"

"Alex." Beth reached over to touch my arm. "You never told me you had all of this going on at work." Her painfully phony interest in me bordered on ridiculous, and I gently pulled my arm away.

"Of course I did. You probably just weren't paying attention." I was sitting between them, a helpless spectator in the middle of their Ping-Pong match.

"Well, anyway," Beth said, looking right through me. It hadn't taken long for me to realize that, although I was the subject of conversation, nothing about this meeting was about me. "What kind of work do you do?"

"I'm an emergency-room nurse, and I work part-time for the park's commissioner." She smiled. "So, Alex tells me you're a bartender at Applebee's?" Point, Michelle.

"Just for now. I'm going back to school soon."

"You are?"

"Yeah, you are?" I echoed in disbelief.

"You knew that, Allie." Her sugary sweet smile made my stomach turn, especially when she put her hand possessively on my knee. Allie? Who the fuck was Allie? She was playing dirty now.

"Allie, huh?" Michelle laughed. "Cute."

"I'll be back. I have to use the restroom." I excused myself and pushed my chair out, suddenly suffocated by the tension, thick like smoke looming in the air.

And then, something happened. Something that made the hairs on my neck stand on end. I returned to find them laughing. And not sociopathic laugher, like Beth was moments away from strangling Michelle, either. This was real, honest-to-God laughter.

"What's so funny?" I asked, afraid to find out. Michelle was wiping the tears from her eyes.

"Beth was just telling me about your trip to Myrtle Beach last year."

"Oh, really?"

"You had such a bad panic attack you had to be pulled off the plane at takeoff?" She began to laugh again, working back to a hysterical roar.

"You told her that, huh?" Beth was playing dirty all right. If she couldn't one-up Michelle with her job, her looks, her life, she could certainly embarrass the hell out of me until Michelle thought I was a loser. If you can't eliminate the threat, manipulate the prize until no one else wants it. I was sick because Beth's true colors were coming to light like I'd never seen. Game. Set. Match.

CHAPTER FIFTEEN

I really like her," Beth said, once we got back that afternoon.
We'd made the ride home in silence, as if she needed time
to reach a verdict on her feelings.

"You do?" I didn't trust her for a second.

"I really do."

"But you were so rude to her," I said.

"I didn't mean to be, Alex. I just got a little insecure. How
could I not? She's beautiful. And really, really great. Who'd
want their wife hanging around with a girl like that?"

"Well, I—"

"I really like her, though. Honestly, I was prepared to hate
her guts." Beth laughed a little.

"That much doesn't surprise me." I grinned back at her.

"I'd like to hang out with her again. You know, the three
of us. Maybe we can go out for dinner later in the week or
something." She was obviously up to something, and it wasn't
looking to make a new best friend either.

"Sure. That'd be...fun." I retreated to the bedroom,
feeling more lost than ever.

❖

Beth hadn't been all talk either, although I'd expected she'd drop the three's company routine in a few days. But sure enough, come Thursday, she was lighting up my desk phone at work.

"Let's go to dinner tonight. Michelle too. Can we, Al?"

"Um, I don't know if she's free. But I can check, I guess."

"Great!"

"Where are you thinking? The bar?" We called Beth's Applebee's "the bar," even when it meant allowing ourselves the luxury of sitting in the actual dining area. It was really the only place we ever went out to eat together, partly because of her hefty employee discount, but mostly because it was familiar and easy.

"No. I was thinking more like Sel de la Terre."

My mouth fell open a hair. "In Providence? That really nice French place?"

"Yes. Why not? Michelle seems like a classy girl who likes that kind of thing." She let just a hint of bitterness sneak out in her tone. "And you're always pissing and moaning that I don't want to do anything sophisticated or whatever."

"Twenty-nine-dollar liver pâté wasn't exactly what I meant," I said.

"Oh, lighten up. And call her. Loveyoubye." She hung up.

What kind of madness was she up to? French dinners? Befriending a sexy, single gay woman who might or might not be secretly vying for my attention? This was not okay. Not okay at all.

I drove home from the office that night still trying to dissect what was surely some kind of master plan on Beth's end. Maybe she was out to make me look completely foolish and undesirable. Or maybe she was planning to seduce Michelle herself, if nothing but for the chance to win her over and then smash her heart into a million tiny shards. Or maybe she really did like her. Maybe she was finally trying to trust me, although somehow, I doubted that.

"Beth? You ready to go?" I called, throwing my coat on the hanger and dropping my briefcase. She didn't answer but instead appeared in the kitchen in a short, black skirt and a low-cut sweater.

"You're going in that?" she asked, gesturing to my office garb.

"You're going in that?"

"What's wrong with what I'm wearing?"

"Nothing. No, it's fine." I was backtracking. "It's just that it's forty degrees out. I'm thinking you might freeze." I *was* worried she might freeze. But I also fought the urge to tell her she looked like some kind of teen Disney star gone skank. I was still angry at her for putting me through this. I didn't want to be having dinner with Michelle while Beth played the good wife just to piss her off. I'd begun to feel like a prize she was out to win, just for the sake of winning.

"I'll go change," she answered.

"Yeah. Me too."

It was Sel de la Terre, after all, so I settled on a tailored blue blazer and slacks that I thought might make Michelle look twice. I don't know why I cared what she thought, but I did.

"Ready," Beth said, posing for me, her miniskirt swapped out for a pair of faded black dress pants.

"That looks nice." Nice. Talk about the least complimentary compliment in the history of the English language. Nice is a way of keeping feelings intact. Nice is what you say when your wife asks how she looks and you can't be bothered to give a damn.

❖

Whoever decided threesomes were so great? Seriously, I want to know. It seems to be every man's ultimate sexual go-to. And probably some women's too. I can't speak for the sex part—that was never on my agenda. But I can tell you that even without the sex, it's a nightmare. I sat at dinner, in between Beth and Michelle, at a square table in a fancy French restaurant in the middle of Providence, thinking I couldn't handle one of them, let alone both.

"Tell me more stories about Alex," Michelle asked Beth.

"Oh, God, I have so many!"

I cut in. "But why spoil all the fun now?"

"She's sensitive." Beth winked, and they laughed together, continuing to pretend to solidify their strange, unlikely bond that was making me uncontrollably frustrated. I wasn't sure who either of them thought they were kidding.

"I've always liked that about her," Michelle responded. There it was, the expected, predictable awkwardness. I blushed hard. Michelle looked uncomfortably at the table once she realized she was flirting. And Beth's face hardened like a tombstone. Twenty minutes into dinner and I already wanted to die.

"Beth, what are you getting to drink?" I finally said, hoping to shatter some of the tension that had paralyzed us.

"I think I'll have a glass of red wine tonight." She smiled at me, a big, manufactured smile that I knew was silently scathing. "How about this? Merlot?" Beth asked, mistakenly pronouncing the "t" at the end. I cringed.

"Good choice," Michelle responded. "They have a great vintage."

"Oh? You know a lot about wine?"

"My grandparents own a winery in Napa," she answered, doing at least a marginal job of keeping her feelings about Beth at bay. The blood between them was clearly bad, and the game was to see who would combust first, leaving the victor the better woman.

"Isn't that…nice." I knew it was only a matter of time before Beth's jealousy and hatred would come to a boil. She was already beginning to simmer. The jig was up.

"You must know a lot about it too, being a bartender and all," Michelle said. "You know, serving all those 'merlots' and all."

I was squirming in my seat.

And here is the problem with threesomes: there's never a balance. Beth had marked me as her territory, if nothing else than just to say she'd won, and she'd do anything to keep Michelle from getting too close. And although I wasn't altogether clear on where Michelle's feelings for me stood, it was more than obvious she wasn't going to let Beth snarl at her either. Beth was like an aggressive dog protecting her food dish, and Michelle wasn't backing down.

"Mostly, we just do beer and mixed drinks." And then, something crazy would happen. Beth's gusto would deflate, just a little, and she would recede, almost defeated. "You know, it's just Applebee's. Not a lot of sophisticated diners there." And I would exhale, thinking I might just survive this dinner yet.

Our conversation was light and airy, albeit it was fake as hell, while we ate. Michelle kept our museum outing and our meetings our secret, and Beth did little else to provoke her. For a short time, I almost enjoyed myself, too. Was it possible to have Michelle as my friend and Beth as my wife? Was that even what I wanted?

"I'll be right back," Beth said, after she finished her chicken. Michelle and I were alone.

"So this is…" I said, trying to find something that described the estrogen-fueled ride we'd been on that night.

"Horrible." And I realized Michelle's face was relaxed for the first time that evening. "Don't get me wrong. I like Beth. A lot, actually."

"You do?"

"Sure I do," she said with forced enthusiasm.

"Really."

"Yes…" She reached out and took my hand across the table. "No." I laughed at her. "Look, Alex. Who are we kidding? We're both adults here, more or less. Can't we just admit that there are feelings here? It doesn't have to mean anything. But it doesn't make it easy to see you with your wife."

My hand shook in hers.

"I had no idea that you—" Beth's emergence from around the corner prompted me to let go.

"That's a really great idea for the Martin case, Alex," Michelle said, loudly. "If you could prove that they were blatantly ignoring data then you'll win for sure." Michelle didn't miss a beat. She never did.

"What are you guys talking about?" Beth sat down again.

"Just this trial I have coming up."

"Tell me about it. I want to hear."

"You do?"

Beth never cared what was happening at work. Law bored her. My job bored her. And I decided the only thing more insufferable than who Beth had become lately was who she was pretending to be.

"Well," I said, "have you heard about the Martin Company? They make some major medications on the market right now. Antidepressants, blood-pressure meds, all kinds of things. Anyway, they conducted a trial to test out a new thyroid medication, and there's a whole group of patients involved in the trial who are suing. They're our clients. They're claiming…" Beth's eyes began to glaze over. *Oh, right. This was why I never talked about work.* "Never mind. It's kind of boring, I guess."

"Are you kidding? It's fascinating!" Michelle defended me, inadvertently touching my shoulder.

"I'm so proud of you, honey." Beth leaned over and kissed my cheek. Her lips were cold and foreign. "I don't know how I bagged myself a lawyer."

Michelle furrowed her brow. "Gee, I don't know either."

The check came without any bloodshed, and I graciously took it.

"Let me pay," Michelle insisted.

"No, no. I've got this." I smiled at her, and for a moment, it was just the two of us.

"Yeah, we've got this," Beth added.

We walked out into the cold night and headed back to Northwood.

"I'm just going to make sure Michelle gets in okay," I said to Beth, once we pulled up into Michelle's house. She eyed me but nodded. I came around and opened the back door.

"I want to finish what we were talking about," I said, quietly, once we'd reached the front door.

"It's not important. Really."

"But it is. It's important to me."

She touched my arm. "Maybe another time then. Good night, Alex. Thanks for dinner." Without another word, she opened the door and disappeared.

❖

I thought for sure our awkward night at Sel de la Terre would have done Beth in. There was no way she'd want to see Michelle again, save maybe to knock out some of her perfect teeth. There was no way she'd let *me* see Michelle again.

But one dinner wasn't enough to derail Beth's scheme to keep Michelle around. And by the time she asked if we could invite her to dinner at our house that weekend, I was sure her motives were more friends-close-enemies-closer than they were prime-time sitcom.

On top of the relationship building among the three of us, work was finally picking up too. I'd been assigned as head attorney to a woman named Joyce Edwards. Her husband, Richard Edwards, was divorcing her after twenty-four years of marriage, and Joyce was out to prove that Richard was unfaithful in order to receive the better part of his assets, which were plentiful, to say the least. Richard owned a condo in the Keys, a ski lodge in Aspen, and two vintage Porsches.

Watson, Johnson and Smith is a corporate law firm, focusing on prosecuting major corporations when the little guy has been wronged. But word had it that Kellen Johnson himself, of Watson, Johnson and Smith, was a close, personal friend of Joyce (I had to wonder how close, exactly. They'd have had to be for the firm to accept a standard money-grubbing divorce suit like this) and had agreed to take her to trial. I knew very little about divorce law and prenups, but Mr. Johnson asked me to be the lead anyway. And when a partner asks you to accept a case, you don't say no. Needless to say, Joyce Edwards held relatively little interest for me.

That was, until she came into my office that afternoon. Joyce was nothing like I'd imagined—a *Real Housewives* platinum-blond boob job in Gucci heels. No. Joyce was a small, stout woman with big, sad eyes hiding behind a few soft wrinkles. She wore a simple pantsuit, and her hair held hints of silver. She approached my desk.

"Mrs. Edwards, I'm Alex Harris." I stood and extended my hand to her. "Take a seat, please."

She didn't speak, her eyes seemingly growing sadder by

the second. It was as if she was afraid to talk, knowing crying wouldn't be far behind. For a long time she sat across from me and studied me.

"You're so young, Alex Harris," she finally said. But it was more of an observation than a criticism.

"I promise you, ma'am, that I'm plenty qualified to take your case."

"Oh, yes, I'm sure. I just meant to say that you're so young because I'm getting so old, and everyone around me seems to get younger and younger. I'm sorry if I offended you."

"Not at all. Now tell me about why you're here."

She was quiet again, evidently collecting her thoughts and pulling the pieces of the last twenty-four years back together.

"We're here because my husband, whom I've been married to since I was twenty years old, wants a divorce. A month ago, he ran off with a tennis pro half his age. How original, right? Bastard doesn't even play tennis. No, he's too fat now to do much more than work and watch TV. But this tennis bimbo wants in on the money. Richard has a successful computer-software company. Now he's saying he wants out, so he can marry the girl in Hawaii." Although Joyce didn't look like I'd expected, her story was sounding like every episode of *Court Television* I'd ever watched in college. This was going to be a chore, at best.

"And what do you need from me?"

"To prove that Richard was sticking it to that twit before he left. I want half of everything. I want the house in the Keys… And I want monthly alimony. Can you make it happen?"

I fought back a groan. "Yes, ma'am. I will try my best. I'll call you in a week or so once I've gone over the PI's report."

She stood and put her coat back on. "Thank you, Alex."

"Take care, Mrs. Edwards." I shook her hand again and she turned to go.

"Alex," she said, turning back to me. "I'm really not a horrible person. I guess I just need to hurt him as much as he's hurting me."

Joyce was gone, but I sat at my desk for a long time, staring at the private investigator's report in front of me. I couldn't shake the pain in her eyes. They were bleeding, heartbroken. Regardless of what Joyce was asking for, all she really wanted was to make the pain stop.

My phone rang, jarring me back to the present. I yanked the receiver to my ear and answered.

"Harris."

"Did you ask Michelle if she can come over tonight?" For a few hours I'd almost forgotten the weird triangle Beth was so set on forming.

"No, Beth. I've been really busy. Besides, maybe tonight isn't a good night. I don't know what time I'll be home."

"Quit whining. I'll call her. What's her number?"

"I don't think tonight's good."

"Just give me her number, Alex. I'll take care of everything. Unless..." Her voice grew dark and heavy.

"Unless what."

"Unless you have some reason not to give me her number. Like maybe you two are hiding something."

"How many more times are we going to do this? We're not hiding anything," I said, my pulse pounding in my temples.

"Good, so then give me her number."

I sighed and gave the phone number to her, afraid of what would happen if I didn't. I hung up, letting my head collapse on my desk in frustration. Maybe Michelle would say no.

Not a chance. Five minutes later, as I was on my way to get my next cup of coffee, the phone clanged again.

"Harris?"

"Did you know your wife just invited me over for dinner tonight?"

"I tried to stop her."

"What is she up to, anyway?"

I sighed again. "Making my life hell."

"You don't think it's possible that she actually likes me, do you?"

"Not likely." We laughed together.

"Good. If she likes me, it means she doesn't see me as a threat."

"Are you a threat?" I asked.

"I think you're the only one who can answer that."

The line went silent for a moment. "Well, anyway, you told her no, right?"

She laughed. "Not a chance in hell. I'll see you tonight, handsome."

I felt like a toy being fought over by two bratty children. I wasn't sure if Michelle was fighting for me or if she was just getting sucked into the games Beth was playing. But as much as I hated the drama their newfound pseudo-friendship was bringing, part of me hoped it was the former.

I couldn't stop thinking about Joyce Edwards on the drive home that night. There was something about the raw sadness that seeped out of her. It was the kind of pain Beth would feel if I left. But then I remembered the condo in the Keys and the alimony, because it was the kind of vicious justice Beth would take. I didn't have any ski condos or vintage cars yet, but what I did have, she would surely try to take if I left. Or maybe I was just a coward, unable to grasp my own happiness out of fear of destroying someone else.

❖

"Honey, you made it home!" Beth greeted me at the door with a long kiss that made the hairs on the back of my neck stand at attention. I flailed my arms, drowning in her shameless attempts to fake a passion that had long since been lost. When she finally came up for air, I saw Michelle, red-faced and hurting, standing next to her.

"I did. Hi, Michelle." I looked them both up and down. Michelle was stunning. But she was always stunning. The shock came from Beth, who wore a form-fitting black lace dress, her chin-length bob parted elegantly to the side. Michelle returned my greeting and hugged me, her cheek just a little too close to mine. It was nearly impossible to pretend I wasn't writhing under her touch, her presence. Her perfume wafted in the air as she moved. Beth cleared her throat. "New dress?" I asked her, unimpressed.

"I did a little shopping today." She giggled and curtsied. "Come sit down. Dinner's almost ready. What can I get you to drink?"

I tried hard not to gawk. Beth had become a Stepford wife herself—the very version of Joyce Edwards I'd expected to walk into my office that afternoon. She was fighting furiously to win a game no one else had signed up for, but the only thing she was accomplishing was looking foolish. Beth poured me a glass of merlot, making a point not to pronounce the "t" this time, and refreshed their glasses as well. God only knew how much wine had gone around before I'd gotten there.

"How was work, Alex?" Michelle asked, after Beth had taken a questionable-looking meatloaf out of the oven.

"Yeah, honey, how was work?" Beth had never called me honey before. But she made sure to look Michelle dead in the eye when she did.

"It was…interesting. I have this new client. She's a forty-four-year-old millionaire. Well, her husband's a millionaire.

And now he wants a divorce so he can marry a twenty-two-year-old tennis pro named Bunny. I'm trying to prove that he was boning Bunny long before he ever told his wife so she can collect."

"I hope you won't say 'boning Bunny' in court," Michelle said, laughing.

"What's wrong with that?" I asked.

"It sounds like something you'd have to get on pay-per-view."

We were both laughing, with Beth chiming in after a few more seconds.

"You're so funny, Allie," she said, taking my hand. "Isn't she funny?"

"She sure is," Michelle answered.

"I'm so lucky," Beth added.

Michelle grew serious, looking into Beth's now conniving, malicious face. "Yes, you really are."

"Let's go to the living room," Beth suggested after we picked at the tepid meatloaf and cold corn. We followed her into the next room, which she'd cleaned more meticulously than I'd ever seen in four years. Michelle and I exchanged a quiet glance behind Beth's back, and I wondered if she wanted me like I wanted her, like my body was on fire just being next to her.

Beth sat on the sofa and insisted I sit there with her, while Michelle took to the only ratty chair in the corner. We sipped on more wine, but Napa didn't produce enough wine to keep me from wishing Beth would disappear. She hung off me in any way she could, draping her arms and legs over me, kissing my face, giggling at everything I said. I tried to pull away, but she would find a way to get on me again, and eventually Michelle's discomfort and dysphoria became more and more evident, until she stood and excused herself.

"It's getting late, and I have to work in the morning," she said. "Thank you both for dinner. It was…nice." Her obvious heartache was the first sign of her I'd seen all night. She was no longer trying to keep Beth from emotionally pouncing on me in order to prove she was the more desirable or likable of the two. The catfight was over. She'd surrendered. She offered a polite smile, and Beth returned a victorious smirk.

I wanted to run to Michelle. I wanted to hold her in my arms and take away any hurt Beth had put there. I wanted to tell her that the only thing Beth had accomplished was further proving just how wrong our marriage was. But I didn't. Of course I didn't. The consequences were too vast. Divorce was too harsh. I couldn't let Beth become Joyce Edwards.

"I'll walk you out," I offered.

Michelle followed me to the door, the despondence now excruciatingly visible in her telltale eyes.

"Thanks, Alex." She kissed my cheek in a way that reminded me of good-bye.

"I'm sorry. Beth, well, she's—"

"She loves you," she said. "That's good enough for me."

CHAPTER SIXTEEN

A week passed without a word from Michelle, although I couldn't say I was surprised. Beth had done her best to alienate her and make her feel like the silver medalist in the Alex Olympics. I was increasingly furious with Beth, who, having accomplished her mission of driving Michelle away, had gone back to her demeaning, miserable ways. But Joyce Edwards was due back to see me, and I'd have to manage to put my petty personal demons to the side.

Sure enough, Joyce was waiting for me when I got to the office at eight thirty a.m. the next Thursday morning.

"Mrs. Edwards. Good to see you again." I opened my office door for her and gestured for her to enter.

"Sorry I'm so early. My sleep schedule has been all thrown off since…Well, anyway, let's just get to it."

Joyce looked tired. More than just the great sadness that engulfed her last time, her eyes were puffy and ringed with dark circles, as if she hadn't seen sleep in months. She exuded a new air of hopelessness, the kind that can only come from giving in to a broken heart.

"I had a chance to review the investigator's report," I said, hoping to infuse some life back into her dead face, "and I think we have some pretty solid proof that Mr. Edwards was… unfaithful during your marriage." I waited for the victory dance. Or the smile. Or something. But all I got was more sadness.

"I've changed my mind."

"You what?"

"I've changed my mind. I don't want anything from Richard. If this is what he really wants, then let's just sign the papers and get it over with."

I sat in disbelief, unsure of what move to make next.

"Mrs. Edwards, you don't have to—"

"I just want to move on with my life. Is that really so wrong?" Her eyes welled with tears.

"No. No, of course it's not." I wanted to reach across the desk and comfort her. "I'll write up the new divorce conditions tonight. I can get this moving pretty quickly."

"Thank you." She dabbed her face with a tissue, got up, and left my office.

So this is divorce. It's not fancy cars or ski condos. It's not even children or retirement funds. It's knowing that the person you gave your life to no longer wants to give you theirs. It's knowing that the person you brushed your teeth next to for the last twenty-four years is tired of it. It's knowing they want someone else. It's heartache. Agony. The ultimate loss.

❖

My desk phone rang for the fiftieth time that hour as I sat at Watson, Johnson and Smith and wrote up Joyce's divorce agreement.

"Harris," I answered gruffly. It was already six on Thursday, and my day was showing no signs of ending anytime soon.

"Is this Alex Harris, of Watson, Johnson and Smith?

Lawyer at large? Big lawyer on campus? Hotshot attorney? Best—"

"Hi, Michelle." I was sure the smile I wore rang in my voice.

"What are you doing?"

"Right now? Just some paperwork."

"What time are you done?"

I scanned the clock on the wall and tapped my pen on the desk anxiously.

"Just a few minutes," I lied. If it meant an invitation to see her, I could make it just a few minutes.

"I need your help with something."

"Oh boy. Last time you asked for my help I ended up in a suit at a stranger's wedding."

She laughed at me. "You're such a whiner. You loved every minute of that."

She was right.

"Okay, so what's your problem now?"

"I bought way too many scallops for dinner."

I smiled to myself. "Sounds like quite the predicament."

"It is...I could freeze them. But they're much better fresh. The only problem is, I don't have anyone to cook them for."

"Is this your sad attempt at a dinner invitation?"

"Is it working?"

I thought about it for a while. I could tell Beth the truth, but she would be at the bar anyway. I was tired of acting like I was doing something wrong. And I was pretty well over our third-wheel routine too.

"I'll be there in half an hour?"

"Can't wait."

I rushed to shut down my computer, waving good-bye to the few employees left in the office. Twenty minutes later, I made it to Michelle's apartment. It was ten minutes before I would actually go in.

Instead, I sat in the front seat, staring at my face in the visor mirror. I tamed a stray hair in the back and layered on some ChapStick, making sure my sweater was still relatively wrinkle-free and not carrying any of the day's coffee on it.

"Don't think I didn't see that." Michelle grinned as she opened the door for me.

"See what?"

"You. Putting your face on. Do I make you nervous all of a sudden or something?"

But she did make me nervous. She terrified me. Maybe she really didn't know the hold she had on me after all. Maybe I didn't even know. I stepped into the kitchen, still trying to decide whether this was a good thing.

She was wearing an oversized wool sweater and tight dark jeans that made it impossible not to stare at her.

"I hope you don't mind my coming alone this time."

"I swear to God, Alex, if I have to watch her hang on you for one more minute…" We laughed.

There were only a couple of years between Michelle and Beth, but it was like they were living in different decades. Beth was disorganized, unmotivated, sloppy. She was lucky to be out of bed by one on most days. If I didn't think of something for dinner, we were eating Lucky Charms with iffy milk. She chose beer over wine, except when she said it made her feel more like a grown-up to do otherwise. Michelle kept seltzer in her fridge and not only ate things like bok choy and brussels sprouts but knew how to cook them too. She spent half of her week making sure people had a place to walk their dogs and play catch, and the other half keeping people from dying. She liked subtitled movies, and I imagined she never let her dirty laundry sit for more than a week. Beth had grown cruel and dark, taking jabs at my job or my family—places she knew would hurt the most. Michelle wasn't perfect. But she knew how to fight fair.

We sat at the small island in the kitchen with nothing but John Coltrane on in the background.

"I'm sorry about the other night," she said.

"Sorry for what?"

"Leaving like that. And then not calling or anything."

"Is that what this is? An apology dinner?" I feigned offense.

"Hardly. This is because I like to cook. And I like to spend time with you."

My face flushed. "You don't owe me an apology. The only one who should be apologizing is Beth."

She cut me off with a polite wave. "She wasn't so bad."

"She was horrid."

"Maybe just a little horrid—"

"I don't know how much longer I can do this…"

"As long as you can," she said stoically, and touched my wedding band the way she had in the café a million months ago.

Michelle made scallops and spinach risotto, and after dinner we ventured to the small living room and watched some Sean Penn movie I was far too distracted to pay attention to. Her hair smelled like wildflowers, and I wanted to put my arm around her and pull her against me. But I didn't.

❖

It was early December, and I had somehow managed to drown myself in the holidays and work just enough to go on like my life hadn't been completely flipped around and scrambled. Beth had been picking up extra shifts at the bar, and I was working six days a week on my next case at the firm. Michelle and I had kept up the routine coffees and bagels, and the occasional homemade dinner or trip to Providence. And Beth, having satisfactorily peed all over me and claimed me as her own, had finally backed off on the idea of the three musketeers, and we'd largely gone back to keeping our distance.

I walked out of the office, greeted by falling snow and storefronts lit with plastic Christmas trees and reindeer. As I took the last icy step from the building, a snowball pegged me in the shoulder, leaving a trail of powder as it broke against me.

"What the hell" I shouted, more than ready to chew out the punk kid who thought this was funny. But I would have recognized the laugh I heard from around the corner anywhere. By the time Michelle peeked her head out, I was already waiting. I hurled the ball of white through the air, missing her by about twenty feet.

"Just what I thought. You throw like a girl," she said.

"Please. I was letting you win."

She came out from her hiding place and stood in front of me.

"Clear your schedule Friday." She reached into her purse and pulled out two tickets I couldn't read.

"And what if I have plans?"

"You don't want to miss this. Fifth row at the symphony. They're doing their holiday show. Wear something nice."

Before I even had a chance to respond, she'd placed the ticket in my gloved hand and disappeared. I walked to my car, smiling the entire way.

CHAPTER SEVENTEEN

Jed was waiting for me when I got home, rubbing my ankles and purring, walking to his empty food dish and then back to me. "Beth? Are you here?" The house was silent. I hung up my coat and dumped a cup of kibble into Jed's dish. "Guess she forgot about us, huh, buddy?" Jed let out a disapproving howl.

The corner of my eye caught Beth's distinctive handwriting, young and flowery, always complete with a spelling error or two. A note was waiting on the counter.

Got called in to work. Be home late.
Love, me

Beth had been working a lot lately—more than ever, actually. I chalked it up to boredom, and maybe even a bit of motivation to contribute a little more to our household income. But it was unusual. In all the years we'd been together, Beth had never sacrificed an evening with me. Not for anything. We were better off apart now, anyway. I brushed off the uneasy feeling her note left me with and sat on the couch, putting my feet up on the coffee table, thinking what would be entirely criminal about calling Michelle. She was the one with the gall to actually show up outside my office and insist I take her to the symphony. Asking for last-minute dinner company seemed pretty benign in comparison. "Don't judge me," I scolded Jed, who was squinting at me from the arm of the sofa.

Michelle answered on the second ring. "You better not be calling to cancel on me already."

"No." I laughed, my nerves easing just a little. "I seem to have found myself home alone with no dinner plans. Any interest?"

"Is that your idea of a proposal?" she said in a low, dramatic voice.

"It's pizza. Not marriage. Are you in or not?"

"Get over here."

"Actually," I said, "you come over here."

"Who is this new, decisive Alex? I think I like her." My heart melted. "I'll see you in a few." The line went dead.

I spent the next fifteen minutes scrambling around the apartment, tossing dirty clothes into hampers and desperately scrubbing at dishes while Jed watched me like I was crazy.

"I hope you like extra anchovies with pineapple," I said, opening the front door for her.

"How did you know?"

"Come in. Let me have your coat."

She followed me into what Beth and I affectionately referred to as the living room, although it couldn't really be called that. It was the size of a nursery and held just our TV, a secondhand couch, and our coffee table with cat scratches up the legs. Michelle's place was nicer, no doubt. Better furnished. Maybe a little bit bigger too. But I wanted her here. I wanted her to be around my life, and my things too.

"So what happened to your dinner plans?" Michelle asked as I opened the steaming pizza box that had just been dropped off.

"They picked up an extra shift at work tonight."

"Her loss. My gain. Now hand over some of that pizza. And it better not actually have anchovies on it."

I gave her a smile and handed her a slice on a paper towel. She took it without question and began to eat.

"Hey, there's a hockey game on. Can we watch?" she asked.

"That's the most beautiful thing any woman's ever said to me."

The heavy snow was piling up fast outside the window, and the traffic on our street had all but disappeared.

Michelle kept an annoyingly appropriate distance between us during the game that threatened to break anything resembling sanity I might have had left. All I wanted was to hold her again. But then, when I held her, all I'd want would be to kiss her. And then all I'd want would be…Well, it would never be enough with her. And I was growing wary of our friendship, wondering how long I could make that enough with her as well.

"It's really coming down out there," she said, somewhere in the third period. "I better get home. I don't want to have to explain to your wife if I get snowed in here."

"She likes you," I answered, awkwardly.

"No, she doesn't."

"Okay, so maybe not…But that's only because I do."

"Well then," she said with a laugh, "I like you too."

"Good."

I smiled at her. "Good."

"All the more reason I don't think Beth would be keen on finding me here alone with you." Her voice sounded off, almost edgy and bitter. "I better dig my car out and get home."

"I'll help."

Her car was already covered in several inches of thick

snow when we got outside. I began to shovel, tossing piles to the side.

"Let me do that."

"Absolutely not," I said, panting.

"Stubborn pain in my ass," she muttered under her breath.

"What did you say?"

"I said," she announced louder this time, "you're a stubborn pain in my ass."

"Just so you know," I picked up a small scoop of snow in the shovel, "you deserve this." I tossed it at her, covering her head and shoulders in white.

"Oh, you jerk!" She squealed and charged at me, smothering my face in it and then pulling my hands away.

"No fair! That was mean!"

We were inches from each other now. I still held her hands. The snow fell around us, sticking to her eyelashes and the ends of her hair and her wool coat. Streetlights highlighted her cheeks with gold.

"You're a sore loser," she whispered nervously, as if afraid to break the quiet that followed the snow. Her arms found their way around my waist. Her warmth seeped through my layers and against my skin.

"You're beautiful…" And I carefully, gently, leaned forward to kiss her.

"Alex, what are you doing?" She gasped, pulling away and pushing me just enough to make her point.

My stomach turned. "I…I don't know."

"You can't do that! You're married! You and I…we're just friends. That's all we ever have been." She took another step back, and my heart plummeted to the ground below.

"But I thought—"

"Well, you thought wrong…I'm sorry."

She jumped into her half-shoveled car, her tires spinning as she pulled away.

❖

I'd never had my heart broken before, but I was pretty sure this was it. I walked around all day with my head to the floor, feeling like stupid, vicious tears were about to attack at any moment. I had no idea what was wrong with me, just that I'd never felt pain like that. I didn't know what any of it meant, and I wasn't sure I wanted to know either. Nothing could have come of whatever I thought had been between Michelle and me. But that was only part of it. Every day I stayed with Beth, I was dying just a little bit more, until the path grew clearer and clearer. Michelle had little to do with it. This was my journey. This was my ending to rectify.

I hadn't heard from Michelle since that night. I wasn't sure I'd ever hear from her again.

CHAPTER EIGHTEEN

My phone rang at ten a.m. on Friday morning, while I sipped a cup of strong coffee and read up on the pharmaceutical company we were suing for manipulating a drug study.

"Harris," I answered, still staring bleary-eyed at the computer screen.

"I take it you didn't look closely at those tickets I got us, did you..." My heart skipped several beats and my head swam. That voice. That perfect voice I thought I might never get to hear again. Without meaning to, Michelle had become my best friend, and the thought of losing her had nearly destroyed me.

"What do you mean?" I asked coolly.

"You're a lawyer. Aren't you supposed to be good with the details?"

And that attitude.

"Get to it, Chatty Cathy."

"The symphony tonight. We're still going, aren't we?" she asked, tentatively.

Were we? I'd been up for two nights straight wondering if she'd ever want to see me again.

"Um. Yeah, sure. Why not?"

"Great! You might want to look at your ticket a little closer then. Can you get out early?"

"The office is closing at noon today. It's supposed to snow later."

"Pick me up at five."

I put down my phone, still trying to figure out what was happening. *The ticket.* I reached into my briefcase and pulled it out.

Boston Pops—Symphony Hall.
Huntington Ave, Boston, MA.

Boston. I laughed aloud to myself until I began to feel as crazy as I knew I must have looked. Shit. Boston. I thought about calling her back, objecting to such a ridiculous idea. But I knew exactly what she'd say—"You're a lawyer. Should have read the fine print." Besides, the idea of getting away from home for the evening felt all too necessary.

I left work a few hours later and headed straight home. The snow was already starting to flurry onto my windshield as I sailed through Northwood, but I didn't care. I had another night with Michelle. Hopefully, I could maintain the guise of friendship for a while longer.

Beth was gone by the time I got home. She'd been picking up doubles at the bar for months now. It was odd. But it also gave me all kinds of freedom I'd never imagined, the best of which being freedom from our constant battles. I changed into a pair of gray wool pants and a maroon sweater and tried to tame my unruly hair. Then I put on my best cologne that Michelle always told me she thought was sexy, left Beth a short note, and took off without looking back.

"I got these for the road," I said when I reached her front door, and handed her a cup of hot coffee.

"You're the best." She took the paper cup and quickly kissed my cheek, leaving a swell of heat where her lips had been. I tried to be grateful that Michelle had kept me an honest wife, but I couldn't help but remember how good those lips had looked just a few nights before.

"So, Boston, huh?"

"Guess we better hit the road if we're going to make it on time." She winked at me and took my arm.

The snow was getting heavier the farther north we drove, but I didn't care. We stopped at a Wendy's drive-thru somewhere across the state line, singing loudly to Christmas songs on the radio. And for an hour or so, I was able to forget she'd completely, unapologetically, turned me down.

"I'm really sorry…about that sad excuse for a kiss."

Michelle looked over at me with a consoling smile. "It's okay. Really."

"No. It wasn't. I don't know what happened to me. I crossed the line. I almost ruined my marriage, and our friendship—"

"But you didn't. Really. It's okay." She reached over and squeezed my shoulder. "And it wasn't sad."

That was it. We kept driving. The snow kept falling. But we didn't say another word about it.

❖

By the time the concert was over, the snow was so heavy that even the lights of the Boston skyline were hazy. The night was unusually quiet, too, with only a few scattered city buses and cabs on the roads.

"This is bad." I looked up to the sky.

"There's no way we're going to make it back to Rhode Island in this." Michelle stopped and faced me. "I think we should stay."

"Stay?"

"Yes. In a hotel? I think they have those here."

A lump formed in my throat and my voice came out in a harsh rasp.

"You want to get a hotel? Together?"

"Well, we could go to separate hotels," she said, lightly punching my arm, "but we'd save money on room service if we didn't."

An entire night, snowed in in some hotel two hours away with Michelle. I could think of worse ways to spend the evening.

"I'll make some calls."

"Okay, big shot." Her smile beamed through the dark.

An hour later, we'd abandoned the car and taken a cab to the Westin by the Charles River. We had no suitcases, no change of clothes, no toothbrush. It was just us and the rest of the night ahead.

I left a message on Beth's cell phone, telling her I wouldn't be home for the night. I tried to be as vague as possible, mumbling something about the storm and a bad connection. And then I hung up. All I could see was Michelle's silhouette, staring out the window into the night. The city cast shadows onto her pale skin and lit up her eyes that were bright with intrigue and awe. Her smile curled at the corners of her mouth, the freckles around her lips still visible in the dim room. Everything around me had fallen to pieces. But as I watched her, the restlessness I'd been fighting for years suddenly settled into the silence. And I knew, as simply, as easily as that, what I was never sure of with Beth.

❖

"I don't feel like going out again," Michelle said. She'd already kicked off her pumps and thrown herself onto the overstuffed king-sized bed. "Let's get room service and order a bad movie. I'm thinking something with Ben Affleck…pre– *Good Will Hunting* days."

My heart was pounding against the walls of my chest so violently it hurt. I stuffed my hands into the pockets of my pants to hide the shaking.

"Sounds good." I moved to the other side of the room and took a cautious seat in a brown leather chair.

Michelle looked at me, uncommonly straight-faced. "Look, Al, if this sleeping arrangement is going to be an issue—"

"It's no problem at all."

But it would be an issue. Because it was all at once as obvious as if it had always been there. I was in love with her.

"Good. Because I was going to say, you could take the floor." She smiled and threw a pillow at me.

"The floor? Not a chance." I threw it back.

"That's what I thought."

The snow continued to fall outside the window, blanketing the city in a perfect white. I couldn't imagine anywhere in the world I'd rather be. We lay on our stomachs, facing the TV, with empty plates and tin covers strewn around the room. We'd cracked a bottle of mini-bar champagne and poured it into hotel-bathroom tumblers. We sipped from them while we watched a God-awful movie, the name of which I will only remember forever because of what the rest of the night would bring.

"I know this probably crosses a lot more boundaries here, but I have to get this dress off." She shifted her legs next to me. "I'm sorry." Was she trying to torture me? Trying to lead me to some unconventional but still brutal death by desire? She got up from the bed and turned away from me, unzipping the dress halfway down her back. "I need some help."

Yes. Death by desire. Goddamn it.

"What? Oh, yeah." I tried futilely to act as if I wasn't jumping out of my own skin. As I pulled the zipper down the rest of the way, I revealed the small of her back and the line of her panties, physically stopping myself from kissing her neck and putting my hands on her. Regardless of what had transpired between Michelle and me, my life as I knew it had just changed forever. My marriage was finished. It had been finished, actually. I was just now strong enough to admit it.

"Thanks," she said shyly, and turned to face me.

She let the dress slip off her shoulders and fall to the ground.

How I kept from touching her in that moment, I'll never know. Neither of us moved. We just stood there, staring at each other, with the lights of the city echoed by snow shining through the big window. I hated her for taunting me. I hated her for making me stand there like an idiot while she undressed. But really, I didn't hate her at all. I loved her. I loved everything about her and everything I saw that night. I loved the freckles on her chest and the lines of her tight stomach. I loved the way she looked at me, as if seeking my approval of her nearly naked body in front of me. And I didn't have it in me to fight it anymore.

"You're welcome," I managed to whisper. My voice was dry and weak.

All she was able to say was my name before she put her hand to the back of my neck and kissed me.

I let myself sink into her as our lips met, slowly at first, then building to a crescendo as if neither of us could get close enough, fast enough. She didn't hold back this time. Her hands yanked my hair, and her mouth probed mine. She ran her tongue around my lips, then pulled away, just for a second.

"I'm tired of pretending." Her words came in breathy gasps. "I'm sorry. I just can't...anymore." Her arms locked around me and she started to kiss me again. I took her face in my hands.

"Stop apologizing."

She pushed her hips into me, her weight covering me until we fell onto the bed. "I've wanted you for so long, Alex."

"Me too. So long..." I kissed her again, tangling my fingers in her long hair as her breathing came heavier.

"I know this is wrong," she said. But I put a hand to her mouth to stop her.

"Don't say anything else..."

Her body rubbed against mine, driving me beyond the point of crazy, until I grabbed her hips and pulled myself on top of her. She kissed my neck, sending waves of heat through me. Her fingers came to the buttons on my shirt, slowing to open them one at a time until I was exposed. I slipped my arms out of the sleeves and returned to her waiting lips.

A quiet moan made its way from her mouth as I kissed a trail from her ear down to her breasts, where I slid the straps of her bra off and took one hard nipple between my fingers. Her hands grabbed furiously at my hair, trying to hang on to what little was there. I reached the black lace panties I'd always imagined her wearing and pulled at the elastic as she raked her nails up my back.

I could feel her eyes on me as I slid the panties down her legs. "God. You're all kinds of sexy," she said. I ran my tongue along the inside of her thighs, stopping only at the small groove where they met her body. "And such a tease... Fuck, I had no idea, Alex..."

When I finally put my mouth on her, she seemed to

have run out of words. I heard only her heavy breathing and incredible, throaty moans that made me feel like I must have been turning her world inside out the way she had mine. Her breathing built in time with her writhing legs, until she was clawing at my neck and my back and my sides.

"Holy shit, Alex." She cried out one more time as her thighs gripped me hard, and then fell, lifelessly.

I stayed there for as long as I could, unable to pull myself up under the spell of just having made love to the most beautiful woman I'd ever seen. She *was* the most beautiful woman too, lying there, smiling and breathless, hair fallen onto the pillow, hands still clenching the sheets. It was the most comfortable, perfect silence I'd ever known. I wasn't thinking. I wasn't wishing I was somewhere else. I wasn't feeling regret or guilt or shame. I was only reveling in the time I was given. And I was overwhelmed by the realization that every minute of the last year had led to this moment. I was exactly where I was supposed to be.

"Come over here and hold me," she said with a newly softened edge to her bossy demeanor I loved so much.

I climbed up the bed until I was lying next to her, my arms circled around her and my eyes on hers.

"Still think I'm predictable?" I whispered.

She laughed softly and stroked my arm. "Yes…I always knew it would be that good."

Chapter Nineteen

I woke up to the sun reflecting off the white snow, shining harshly into the hotel room. Michelle was still in my arms, breathing gently against my skin. I didn't want to wake her. I wanted to hold on to the feeling of her weight against my body as long as I could. Because, really, I didn't know if I'd ever get to feel it again.

She let out a small moan and turned her head until she was looking at me.

"You're up," she said, her eyes still heavy and her smile missing its usual gleam.

"So are you." I kissed the top of her head and rubbed her bare back. I would make sure to never forget how she felt. I would make sure to never forget any of this.

"Looks like the snow stopped. We should probably get home." Breaking the spell we'd been held under, she sprang out of bed, sheet wrapped around her, and began the search for her missing clothes. Disappointment snuck up on me again. I could feel her pulling away. I could feel the night dissolving around us.

I dropped Michelle off at home, and with nothing more than a simple kiss on my cheek, she opened the door and left.

❖

On Tuesday, I went to the café, but Michelle wasn't there. I had no sassy phone calls, no surprise visits to the office. The silence was lethal. And deafening. My real life had never seemed so loud before without the lull of her presence in my day to dampen it. It was just me now. Well, me and Beth. But it couldn't be us any longer. I had to tell her.

"You're home." Beth greeted me flatly.

"Yeah, I left work a little early today."

"That's good." She opened the fridge and popped a bottle of beer.

"Beth, listen, I need to talk to you…" My pulse exploded. This was the beginning of the end. Or maybe it would be the beginning of something else entirely.

"I was just headed out to do some Christmas shopping." She sat down on the stool at the breakfast bar, her eyes darting around the room nervously. "Come with me."

"We really need to talk about something—"

"When we get back. Just come with me. I could use some company."

I wanted to object. But if I didn't go with her, I might never find the nerve to tell her again.

"Sure. Let's go."

Beth and I drove to Providence. The trees outside the shopping area were covered in snow and lights, and excited kids chased their siblings through the aisles of the stores. Christmas was only a week away. This was normally my favorite season. This year, though, I was torn between a devastating sense of loss and a chance to start again. Which feeling weighed heavier seemed to depend on the moment.

"What's wrong with you, Scrooge?" Beth was teasing me.

"Beth, we really need to talk—"

"I have an idea. Come on. It'll only take a minute."

She wasn't going to make this easy. And her sudden Christmas spirit sent waves of uneasiness through me.

"Fine. Okay. But I mean it. I want to talk about this."

I followed her back to the car, carrying our bags of gifts, and got in the passenger seat.

"What are we doing?" I stared out the window.

"It's a surprise." I wasn't sure why she was being so nice to me. Her sugary falseness reeked of guilt.

I thought about Michelle. "White Christmas" played low on the radio as Beth drove, and my heart continued to break—— for the loss of my marriage, for the loss of love that never was, and for the loss of my two best friends. What I didn't realize about broken hearts, having never really had one until now, was that it's not a one-time deal. A broken heart happens over and over again. That first break? That's just the beginning, until you can't even hear a goddamn Christmas song on the radio without tearing up. Is this what I'd been doing to the girls I dated years ago? Because this was agony.

A few minutes later, we pulled down a dirt road I'd known well at one point.

"I'm guessing you've figured it out by now," Beth said, as she pulled up to the skating rink. "This always makes you feel better. No matter what's bugging you."

When I was ten, my parents finally agreed to let me play hockey, although my dad hated that it was a "boy sport" and made me do yard work all summer just to save enough for my gear. My mom drove me to my first practice, which, at that age, entailed a lot of bumping into each other on the ice. But I loved it. It was the only place I'd found so far where I didn't have to be someone I wasn't. My dad never did come to a game, even though I played all through high school. I guess that should have been a harbinger for our future bond—which wasn't much. But every time I laced up my skates and drove back to that same rink, I was ten again, with nothing to think about except where the puck was. Beth knew all this.

It wasn't perfect. We were broken, and lost, and hopeless. The end had come, and on some level, we both knew it. But for an hour, if only an hour, we raced around the ice as carols blared through muffled speakers, and time was frozen. Nothing was going to change. But for just a drop in the bucket of our lives together, we could just be. And after a while, I heard a sound I hadn't heard in almost a week: my own laughter. Beth chased me like we were children, finally catching me and pushing me a little before she'd skate off.

For a minute, it was hard to forget the good in her. The good that had been between us was gone, but I wouldn't allow myself to completely dismiss what had once been.

A week before our first Christmas together, my dad had been forced to put our cat, Henry, down. We'd had him for seventeen years—most of my life, really—and he was my best friend in the world growing up. He got old, though, as animals always do, and sick. And come that December, his kidneys were shutting down and he was miserable. My dad did the humane thing for Henry, but I was a mess. I cried for days when he died. Then, on Christmas Day, I woke up to a tiny "mew" and a cold nose on my chin.

"He's Henry Two," Beth had said, placing the little orange kitten in my arms. She'd driven five towns over in the middle of the night on Christmas Eve to get him.

We'd had our good times—lots of them. I'd made the choice that would save us both. For tonight, I'd remember loving her for everything she'd done for me and everything she'd been to me. I loved her for helping me grow, even in our stagnancy. I loved her for being my best friend, who knew I needed nothing more than to glide in circles to "Let it Snow." Some things, even time won't erase.

❖

I wished those memories and distant longing would have been enough. But that wasn't reality. Reality was that Henry Two was tragically hit by a car the next year. Reality was that one evening of ice-skating and hot cocoa couldn't repair years of misplaced affections and endless pain. Nothing could.

"That was fun," Beth said, crashing onto the couch.

"Beth—"

"Just say it Alex. Tell me you want to leave."

She knew all along.

"I—"

"Say it. We both know it's true." Her tone was steady and chilling.

"This isn't working." I exhaled, years of confusion and angst flowing out with the air.

"How can you say that? Tonight was—"

"Tonight was just one night. One night out of hundreds. That's not enough."

Her eyes welled with tears. "You don't mean that."

"I do. And you know it's true too." I tenderly brushed her cheek.

"But…I love you…"

My heart split to pieces in my chest. I knew how much I'd hate hurting her. What I didn't realize was how much I'd be hurting myself.

"I'm sorry…I'm so sorry…"

❖

No breakup is truly amicable. One person always wants it more than the other. But Beth somehow found it in her to let me sleep on the couch until I could find somewhere else to go. She was hurt and angry—crushed even. We both were. But even she knew we were headed for something better. No one wants to get divorced. No one gets married thinking "this will do for now." I'd failed, and I'd lost. I'd lost my marriage, the life we'd built, and the person who'd been my companion for the last four years, even when the seas had gotten rough. Some nights, alone on the couch with nothing but the company of Jed and late-night TV, I'd cry until I didn't think any tears were left in me. And then I'd cry some more. But I'd always wake up bathed in a sense of possibility and relief. If I could just get through the pain, I'd come out better for it. And I knew Beth would too.

It was also hard to forget that Michelle hadn't spoken to me. And it was devastating. I thought about her nearly every second of every day. In the days leading up to Christmas, I'd seriously considered calling her. But I always stopped myself before the call ever connected. I told myself it was better this way—that I was in no condition to love anybody right now.

A week passed. Then two. And instead of getting better, I was doing the opposite, struggling for normalcy with a broken heart I couldn't speak with anyone about. Beth and I weren't talking. We merely passed by each other in our travels, like acquaintances who hardly knew each other.

Time, and pain, got the best of me, and I called Michelle. And when she didn't answer, I called again. I sent a text message. And then another. And finally, in my last and most pathetic attempt, I sent a bouquet of lilies you couldn't even get in New England this time of year to Northwood Hospital. But I was met with cold, debilitating silence. I taunted myself with the impossible questions—was she just scared? Or maybe I was just really shitty in the sack? Maybe that was it. Maybe I'd become so sexually inept over my years of near marital celibacy that I'd completely forgotten how to fuck a woman. It was possible, no, it was likely, that Michelle had woken up that morning from a sort of *Coyote Ugly* moment, wishing she could chew her own arm off so she didn't have to face me. The ultimate walk of shame. The ultimate regret. Or maybe I just no longer deserved the kind of love I felt for her.

Sure, I could contemplate those answers all day. I was getting pretty creative with them too. But truth be known, Michelle took those answers with her when she vanished. And I'd probably never know what went wrong.

❖

It was Christmas Eve—normally my second-favorite day of the year, after the big day itself. When we were kids, my parents always made a big thing of it. The morning started with a large breakfast, complete with eggs and pancakes, and a grilled cheese for my brother, who hated breakfast. We went to the early church service together, where we lit candles and sang "O Holy Night." And then we opened stockings and drank eggnog by the tree my dad worked so hard to perfect. We kept up most of those traditions for years, although my brother still won't touch eggs.

But when Beth and I got married, I inherited a new family and began to make a family of my own as well. We split the holidays between hers and mine, as we frantically tried to make something our own over the years. This year, I had no family. I had nothing except my stacks of cases, a ratty blanket on our sofa, and the comforting sense that I'd finally done the right thing.

I woke up that morning to a crash in the kitchen. Beth was

at the stove, swearing under her breath at a saucepan that had fallen and hit her bare foot.

"What are you doing?" I asked cautiously, trying to hide my surprise.

"What's it look like? I'm making you breakfast."

I couldn't help but smile. "But…why?"

"It's Christmas Eve. Why not? Besides, we both need to eat." She returned a small smile, and I wondered if someday, when the wounds healed a little, we could find a way to be something again.

A flood of hot, sudden tears rushed my eyes and blinded me. I grabbed Beth around the shoulders and hugged her as hard as I could manage. Her body was stiff and uncertain, but she didn't fight it either.

"Thanks, Beth." I sniffled into the shoulder of the now-threadbare UCLA sweatshirt she still wore. "But next time, you don't have to use that heavy saucepan. Those things kill when they land on you."

She laughed. "I'll keep that in mind."

"I know this doesn't mean you're forgiving me or anything…I just…"

"It's only breakfast, Alex. Really."

A peace that hadn't existed between us in years fell over us. We ate our scrambled eggs in front of the Christmas special on ABC.

"I want you to have your present," I said, not really sure why. She looked at me hesitantly as I handed her a small, poorly wrapped package. Beth opened the box and took out a necklace with a small silver key on it. "I bought it a while ago, and I just…I want you to have it."

"It's gorgeous."

"I thought it looked like you."

"Alex, I…" Her eyes became wet, but there was no smile behind them like there was mine.

"I'm sorry. I'm so sorry I hurt you. I promise this is going to be the best thing for both of us." I moved to her side and put my arms around her.

"I've been cheating on you." As soon as she spit the words out, she burst out into loud, violent sobs. My mouth hung open.

"You what?"

She was still crying uncontrollably into my neck.

"I…" She wailed. "I've been with someone else."

I pulled away, my head suddenly cloudy. "With who, Beth?"

"A customer…" She gasped. "It was"—*gasp*— "nothing…" *Sob*.

I took her face into my hands and forced her to look at me. "What do you mean?"

She pulled herself together enough to look at me, but she was still sniffling and shaking dramatically. "She's a customer at the bar. I was lonely. We were fighting all the time. You said it yourself—we weren't happy. Besides, none of this really matters now, does it?"

"I…I have to go…" I shook my head, rising to my feet. I got my coat and walked out the door.

I flew out of the driveway and down the road, not sure where I was going or what I was doing. The streets underneath me were slick, and the rear of my car slid from side to side. I heard a satisfying crunch under the tires as I regained control again. Fury like I'd never felt was pulsing through me. It was all at once unjustified and blinding. She'd only done to me exactly what I'd done to her. I yanked my hands off the steering wheel and pulled at my wedding ring. When it was finally off, I opened the window and let the cold wind carry it away.

The anger was so bright that it blended into the headlights that were coming straight at me. The glass shattered in a single, screeching blow. Then, the light was gone.

CHAPTER TWENTY

A new light, not quite as bright as before, replaced the darkness that had consumed me, though it was still strong enough to cause a rippling pain in my head.

"Can you hear me? You're in the ambulance," a voice said from somewhere above me. My eyes slowly began to focus as two guys in blue emerged. Something was squeezing my arm, hard, and tubes and wires were leaving or entering my body, in one way or another —I couldn't tell which. Bells screamed in the distance somewhere. "You were in an accident," one of the men said. The bells screamed louder. "Blood pressure is 85/50. Pulse is up to 120."

"Let's step on it a little."

But I was out again.

❖

"Alex. Alex, you bastard, wake up." I woke to my name being called over and over, often accompanied by some kind of expletive. The back of my head throbbed with every heartbeat, and I was blanketed in a sheet of ice, in spite of the warm room. Another bright light was beaming over me. *Enough with the damn lights already!* A dull ache raged inside my chest. As hard as I tried to open my eyes, I couldn't clear the layer of fog that lay over them. The voice continued to call my name. Beth? No. At least, I hoped not.

Days must have passed. Or it could have been minutes. I had no idea. Finally, I was strong enough to force my eyelids open. I strained to focus, the throbbing in my head getting worse by the second. It was getting harder to breathe, too. I tried to look around the room, but something kept my neck stiff. Someone stood over me, her face obscured by the shadows of the big white light overhead.

"There you are!" she said. I couldn't make her out through the clouds. But I knew the hand that was brushing my face.

"Michelle?" My voice crackled. My tongue was hot, and I could feel dried blood on my cheek.

"It's me. I'm here. I'm right here…"

❖

When I woke up again, it was dark. The pain in my head was letting up just a little, and a warm body was curled up against me. I could smell wildflowers, even through what I was guessing was a busted nose, and my hand, still wrapped in tape with tubes snaking from it, had someone's fingers gently grasping it. Those fingers—I knew those fingers. They were the long, soft fingers that had combed through my hair as I kissed down her smooth stomach. They were the fingers that lit a fire in me when they were close.

"Michelle," I mumbled. My mouth was like sand, and my muscles felt weak just from talking. She lifted her head from my chest, where she'd obviously fallen asleep.

"Hi." She smiled sweetly and put her hand on my stomach. "Don't you think you've slept long enough?"

I managed to return a weak smile. "What happened?"

She stroked my hair. "You were in an accident. A bad one."

Pieces of that morning, or whatever time of day it had been, inched back slowly. I remembered the anger, the betrayal from both of us. I remembered the tires against the ice. And I remembered the pain.

"Am I going to die?" I said, tearfully.

Michelle laughed. "No, sissy-pants, you aren't going to die." She curled up against me again and stroked my stomach over the thin hospital johnny. "Some dumb-ass crossed the center line. You hit the steering wheel pretty hard, and your car's totaled. But you're going to be okay."

"Why are you here?"

She laughed again. "I work here. Remember? And you've been making my job very difficult today."

"Beth…" I whispered.

"I know. I'll call her. I was just waiting until—"

"Don't…" I rasped, trying fruitlessly to sit up.

"Hey! It's okay, Al! Just relax." She was smoothing my hair again. The pain was overwhelming, this time spreading from the top of my head to my toes. Every hair on my body hurt. Someone else entered the room.

"I've got some more Dilaudid for her," the voice said to Michelle, and someone began to pull at the tubing leaving my hand.

"Don't call Beth," I managed to say, before the world once again closed in on me.

❖

I had no concept of what time it was, only that the sun was streaming through the windows of the room I was in, leaving a blistering heat on my face. My left hand was being caressed, someone softly stroking my ring finger.

"Your ring," Michelle said, softly. "You must have lost it somewhere—"

"I didn't lose it." My voice was stronger now—stronger than it had ever been, actually. "I threw it out the car window."

Her laughter built slowly, starting hesitantly at first and rising to an uproar that brought me with it.

"What?" she asked, still bellowing.

"Stop! It hurts to laugh." I gritted my teeth a little, but I was still smiling.

"I'm serious, Alex. Where's your ring?"

"I'm serious too. I threw it out the window. It's probably sitting on Hobarth and West somewhere in a snowbank. It'll make some homeless person very happy."

"You and I both know there are no homeless people in Northwood."

"It's over." It felt strange to say it aloud, like the words couldn't possibly be my own. Never in four thousand different endings did I imagine this.

"Alex, I'm…" She stopped, as if to reconsider. "I'm sorry things didn't work out."

"She cheated. We both cheated, I guess. It's been over for a long time now, I think."

She was poised and reflective. "You did the right thing."

"That's about the only thing I'm sure of these days."

A handsome figure appeared in the doorway, but it took me a moment to place her through the fog of medication and pain.

"Alex, how are you feeling?" Charlie asked. I recognized that charisma and confidence from the wedding.

"I'm okay. Still sore."

Charlie moved to the bedside. "Good. I'm just going to do a quick exam here."

"I'm going to grab a coffee. You want anything, Charlie?" Michelle asked.

"Just a Diet Coke. And a black coffee for Nat, if you don't mind."

Michelle nodded.

"Thanks."

Charlie's face grew stern and serious with Michelle's exit, the tender doctor with the boyish charm quickly replaced by nothing but business. She wiggled her fingers in front of my eyes and asked me to follow the light on the end of her pen.

"No head injury. Your scans all look good. You broke your clavicle in three places, but other than that I'd say you're pretty lucky."

"Lucky…Right."

"Yeah…Lucky, Alex. Don't blow it." And somehow, I had a feeling we weren't talking about my driving any longer.

❖

I was moved to a room on the third floor later in the day, and Michelle refused to leave my side, except to run down the street to my favorite sub shop in town and get me the biggest pastrami-and-pickle sandwich they made.

"Pastrami, pickles, no veggies, extra mustard for you, and a nice, healthy tuna sandwich on wheat for me." She was teasing me as she dropped the food onto my bedside table.

"You're the best."

"I also brought some trashy celebrity magazines and a deck of cards. And if you're really good, I know where they keep the ice cream up here." She winked at me.

"Can you please take care of me forever?"

"God knows you need it."

We ate our sandwiches in between criticisms of the latest episode of *The Bachelor*, and when she was finished, she got into bed beside me and put her arms around me.

"I have to admit, I've had worse days than this," I said.

"Worse days than a fractured clavicle?"

"Yeah. You're here. That makes the rest of it okay."

❖

Michelle had to go to back to work in the Emergency Room the next morning, although she offered to call out again. Another nurse took over my care—a much older, meaner one named Pat, who didn't look nearly as good in a pair of scrub pants. I missed Michelle. It hadn't taken long to get used to having her around every second I could. And her unrequited feelings did little to settle how in love with her I really was.

"Here're your meds," Pat barked, handing me a small plastic shot glass filled with massive horse pills. "Oh, and you have a visitor."

I had no idea who it could be, since once I'd realized I wasn't going to die, I'd opted not to tell my estranged parents. Although they'd come to the wedding, they were never really sold on the whole gay thing, or Beth, actually. We hadn't talked much over the last few years.

The white-haired, grumpy Pat left the room, and a few minutes later the curtain slid open again, leaving a grating sound in its wake.

"Oh my God! I just heard!" Beth rushed to my bed and threw herself on top of me. "I would have come sooner, but I had no idea what had happened!"

"Beth. What are you doing here?"

"What do you mean? I was so worried." She brushed my hair with her fingers, and I squirmed underneath her touch.

"I told them not to call you. How did you know?"

"Some doctor named Dr. Thompson told me you were here."

"Fucking Charlie..." I mumbled.

The curtain squeaked one more time, and in walked Michelle, brow furrowed, determination in her step.

"What's she doing here?" they asked in scripted stereo. Why was it that every time the two of them got together, I found myself stuck in the middle of a poorly written sitcom?

"Why don't you ask your friend Charlie," I said gruffly.

"I want you to leave," Michelle said, bypassing me completely and zeroing in on Beth.

"I'm her wife. And I don't think that's up to you."

Michelle's eyes narrowed. "I don't think you get to call yourself her wife anymore."

"Who the hell do you think you are, anyway? You're just some whore who tried to steal Alex."

"Excuse me?" I could almost see the smoke billowing from Michelle's ears.

"I told you, Beth. It's over between us. I thought you understood—"

"I never tried to steal your wife," Michelle said. "Don't go projecting your own infidelity on me. Or should I use smaller words that you might understand better?"

"Alex, will you please tell your skank to leave?" Beth asked.

"I think you should be the one to leave," I said, once they finally allowed me to speak. Beth looked at me, wounded, but I felt nothing.

"You heard her," Michelle said. "Go, before I call security."

Beth gave one last pout and left, defeated.

❖

I awoke later that night to the sound of Michelle's voice outside my hospital room. At first I swore I was still dreaming. I'd had a million dreams with her voice in them.

"You're being a jerk."

"I am not. I'm just looking out for you." I knew that voice too, although not nearly as well, and not for the same reason. It was husky and serious, and full of what sounded like true concern for her.

"Well, you don't have to look out for me, Charlie. I'm not a kid."

"You're acting like one. You're going to get hurt."

"So what? Now that you're married you think you know everything?"

I sat up as quietly as I could, trying not to so much as rustle the bedsheets as I made my way to the door. My hospital socks stuck to the floor, and my legs shook underneath me. I made it to the curtain, hiding behind it while I peered into the bright hallway. Michelle stood nose to nose with Charlie, her face fierce.

"I don't know everything," Charlie said. "But I do know you're cruising to get your heart broken."

"Just like you did to me?"

"This is nothing like that and you know it." I watched Charlie's face turn crimson, contrasting to the sharp white of her lab coat.

"No, it's not. But you know what it is like? It's like this young doctor I know, who met her wife. You see, it's kind of a funny story, because her wife was actually, get this, married to someone else." Michelle let out a sarcastic cackle.

"Michelle."

"Wait, this is good. So, this young doctor fell in love with this other doctor, but she was already married! Can you believe it? And, as the story goes, they still fucked each other senseless. The nerve! And you know what happened next, Charlie?" Charlie looked nervously down the halls as Michelle raised her voice. "She left her husband. And the young doctor got to marry her. Now how about that for a happy fucking ending?"

"Are you done?"

"I think so." Michelle huffed.

"You are not me. And Alex is certainly not Natalie. This girl is married, and she's playing with you. And you're going to get hurt."

"You're wrong about that part. I'm not going to get hurt because Alex is my friend. And unlike you, I don't chase married women."

She nearly took me out as she stormed back into my room, barreling through the curtain. I managed to dive back into the bed, slamming my already shattered shoulder on the rail as I did.

"You okay?" she asked, sitting down next to me.

"Oh yeah," I said between gritted teeth, but the pain was raging.

"You're breathing fast and your face is all red. Here, let me take a look at you."

She raised her hand to touch me, but I quickly pushed it away. "I'm okay. Really."

"Alex. Stop being a pain in the ass and let me check you out." She put two fingers to my wrist and looked at the clock on the wall, seemingly satisfied I was all right.

I was quiet for a long time. "Where did you go?" I finally asked.

She gently took my hand and held it to her face. "I didn't go anywhere."

"Yes, you did. After things happened...after we happened...you were just...gone."

Her eyes became thick with pain I hadn't seen since she talked about Charlie.

"It was a mistake. All of it."

"A mistake? No." I was growing stronger now, frustration and disappointment bringing me out of my fog. "No. I don't buy that for a second."

"I'm sorry." Her tone was frigid and stoic.

"Sorry? Bullshit. You felt something. You still feel something. This is real. And you're just scared."

A nurse dressed in blue scrubs appeared in the room. "Everything okay in here?"

"We're fine," Michelle answered. "I was just leaving."

And I was alone. Just me, the nurse in the blue scrubs, and the pain.

CHAPTER TWENTY-ONE

Michelle didn't come back. Neither did Beth. A few days later, I was discharged with nothing but a Vicodin prescription and a bag of bloodstained clothes. I didn't know where I was going to go. I just knew it wouldn't be that place I used to call home.

I searched the hospital parking lot for at least twenty minutes, trying to remember where I'd parked my car. *Right. Totaled.* Embarrassed and defeated, I called the only cab company in Northwood.

"Where to?" the driver asked, a half-smoked cigarette hanging out of his mouth. Where *to? Great question.* I could sleep at my desk for a few days until I got my act together. I could get a hotel room. I could take a bus to my parents' in New Hampshire. But none of that seemed at all tolerable. "Where you going, kid?"

Before I could stop myself, I'd climbed in the backseat and was giving him Michelle's address.

Five minutes later, the cab pulled up to her place.

"Oh, for Christ sake," Michelle exclaimed, throwing her arms in the air and walking out into the cold. "Who said you could go home?"

She rushed to my side, wearing nothing but a pair of slippers made to look like cats and a tattered sweatshirt and shorts. It was a leap from her usual heels and red lips, and something about her appearance made my heart erupt in my already bruised chest.

"Nice slippers." I smiled weakly at her as she wrapped her arm around my waist and helped me to the door.

"You look like a beaten puppy," she teased me, guiding me to the couch. "Pathetic."

"I'm sorry. I just didn't know where else to go."

Michelle picked up a blanket and covered my lap before sitting beside me. "Of course you can come here, Alex."

"I just can't go home again."

"I know." She pulled up a corner of the blanket and tucked herself under it, moving in closer to me. "You don't have to."

❖

I must have fallen asleep again, because the next thing I remembered was the sound of metal clanking together in the kitchen. But it was the smell that woke me—some kind of medley of garlic and parsley and spices I couldn't identify because I was no kind of cook. Michelle walked in, a blue-plaid apron tied tightly around a much sexier version of the earlier day's outfit. The shorts were shorter and did everything they could to show off her mile-long legs, and a revealing tank that did little to hide her full breasts had replaced the sloppy sweatshirt. "You did that on purpose, you tease…" I mumbled to myself.

"Morning, sunshine." She smiled.

"What time is it?"

"Seven thirty at night." Music was coming from the other room—something that sounded like old Eartha Kitt—but she'd left the TV on low for me in the living room while I slept.

"How long have I been out?" I was still groggy as I sat up, wincing at a sharp pain ravaging my back.

"A few hours. Dinner's almost ready. I hope you like homemade Italian red sauce."

"Hate it." I wiped the sleep out of my eyes.

"Too bad. Chef's choice." She left the room again and returned with a gym bag—my gym bag.

"What's that?"

"Your things. I hope you don't mind too much. While you were sleeping I took your keys and went to grab some of them."

I deliberated for a minute, trying to decide if she was criminal or incredible, or some crazy concoction of both. "You broke into my house?"

"I wouldn't say that. I just wanted to make sure you had something to wear while you're here."

While I'm here. I liked the way that sounded. I was battered and bruised, and felt like a boulder was parked on my head, but if it meant bunking with Michelle, I'd have gladly been in five more accidents.

"Was Beth there?"

"No. Don't worry. I'm going to finish dinner. Don't you even think about moving from that couch."

She must have taken off the hospital johnny and scrub pants I'd come home in, because when I finally looked down at myself, I realized I was wearing only a white undershirt and my briefs. My gym bag was just a few feet away, but it was going to take every once of strength I had left to get to it.

"I thought I told you not to move." Michelle stood in the doorway again, smiling, her hands on her perfect, curvy hips. I stumbled back to the couch again while she rummaged through the bag and threw me a pair of sweatpants. "Here."

"Is this what I get when I crash here? Nurse Michelle?"

"Oh yes. And I can get very bossy."

She left the room and returned a moment later with two plates covered in pasta and eggplant and sauce.

"You have no idea how good this smells," I said.

"You've never had sauce like this. I promise. Made by a full-blooded Italian."

"Masters isn't Italian, is it?"

She chuckled at me. "No, definitely not. But Ricci is." I looked at her blankly. "Masters isn't my real name. When I was five, my mom gave me up. She was a junkie, and so Auntie Judy and Uncle Walt raised me. My mom was a Ricci."

"And she taught you how to cook?"

"No. When I was little, my aunt used to let me stand on one of those little stools in the kitchen and help her stir."

She was smiling at the memory, somewhere inside of herself.

"Well worth it. This is unbelievable."

"You're just saying that because you can't even follow the instructions on the back of a pack of Easy Mac."

"You'd be amazed what I can get away with, with these looks."

"Trust me. I've noticed." Her eyes were hazy as they caught mine, lust and need and ruthless want flooding them. I knew that look. No matter what her words said, I knew that expression.

But instead of kissing me, like she had in the hotel, she broke the stare and turned on the TV and started flipping through the channels.

We finished our dinners as we watched the end of the Bruins game, but just like everything else, it was different with Michelle. TV after dinner didn't feel like a way to avoid bland conversation or a passionless romance. It felt like comfort, and home, and love. It felt like the life I'd always wanted.

Michelle took our plates to the kitchen. There were two other chairs in the living room, but she sat in the spot beside me, right in the middle of the sofa. I lifted my arm as she did, and she collapsed into me, nuzzling her head against my chest. Her body was warm against mine, and I tried hard not to think about how good she felt.

"Am I hurting you?" she asked, her voice suddenly heavy with concern.

"Not at all." The building pressure where she was lying was blunted by the tingling through the rest of my body that I always felt when she was touching me. For years, I'd settled for less with Beth. And maybe, now that Michelle had drawn the friend line with us, I was settling again. But I couldn't pull away—not when she felt so soft and wonderful. Not when I had everything I wanted, even if it was just for a little while.

The pain pill Michelle had given me was kicking in, and it was getting harder to keep my eyes open. Finally, I gave in, letting myself drift off to sleep with Michelle at my side.

❖

A bang at the door the next morning dragged me out of my Vicodin-fueled doze. Michelle trotted out from the other room.

"Where is she?" I recognized that voice instantly, although I couldn't see who was standing there. It was a voice ravaged with desperation and heartache—one I'd spent four years with. It was the voice she used whenever I threatened to walk away, whenever I wanted to leave her.

"Can I help you?" Michelle was calm, completely unfazed by Beth's presence.

"I know she's here. I need to talk to her."

I scraped myself up and got to my unsteady feet. "What do you want, Beth?" It took a while, but eventually I limped to the door.

"I just want to talk to you." She pushed her way past Michelle into the apartment.

"How did you find me anyway?"

"You left her address on a pizza receipt in the bedroom, you moron." But she wasn't angry. "How long has this been going on? You two, I mean?"

"I'm fine, by the way. Thanks for asking. Major car accident. No big deal," I said.

"I was getting there. Can I sit down?"

"Sure. I was just on my way out." Before I could stop her, Michelle was out the door, and I was alone in the living room with Beth.

"Why are you here?"

She put her arms gently around my waist, like I was fragile, breakable. But I wasn't. Not anymore. I was bruised and a little worn, but definitely not breakable. I pulled away.

"I want to fix this."

I laughed sarcastically and looked away.

"I mean it. We were both wrong. I cheated, you cheated. Let's just move on."

She couldn't be serious. "Did you skip that day in third grade when they tell you two wrongs don't make a right? Don't you think there's a reason both of us couldn't stay faithful after only three years?"

"I was wrong. I'm so sorry. She meant nothing to me. Let's just call it even."

"You're kidding me, right?" I was angry again, willing her

with my vicious glare to get out of my sight, out of Michelle's apartment.

"I think we can make it." She fell to her knees in front of me.

"You don't want that. I don't want that. It's over."

She got to her feet. "Alex. Please."

"Good-bye, Beth."

She watched me for a long time, crying, testing my resolve. How many other times had I wanted to leave, only to turn back at the thought of an insufferable divorce? At the thought of being alone? Not this time. When I didn't budge, she turned and left.

After the door had closed behind her, I allowed myself to fall apart, angry tears streaking down my face. I was a failure. Three years of marriage, and I was walking away. Just another statistic. I'd done exactly what I swore I'd never do.

I was still wrapped in a cloak of self-pity when Michelle came home, carrying a paper bag and two paper coffee cups. She didn't say a word. She just put down the groceries and sat by me, holding me while I cried.

"I brought you a bagel with jam," she said, finally, pulling away from me and lifting my chin. "It's from the café."

I'd never been a crier. The only time I remember crying much was when Henry died. It never seemed to do much of anything for me. But I couldn't stop. I felt like twenty-nine years' worth of feelings were tumbling out of me and onto the couch cushions. I was no longer crying for Beth. I wasn't even crying because I was sad. I was crying because I'd never felt such relief. I was a clean slate. Everything could start over. And I'd be damned if I wouldn't do it right the next time.

"I'm sorry for being such a baby," I said, humiliated by my blatant vomiting of emotions.

"I had no idea you were such a softie."

"I'm not. I swear."

"Alex," she put her hand to my cheek, "if there's ever a reason to be a softie, it's losing your wife."

"That's not it. I'm just...I feel like I set myself free."

"You did."

I was quiet for a while, taking in the lines of her eyes and the tiny point of her nose. Even if she could never love me the way I'd fallen in love with her, at least I'd finally learned how.

"I don't regret it," I blurted out. "I don't regret us. I know it was just one night, but it was the best night of my life. And I refuse to regret it. I'm sorry, but I just don't."

"I never signed up to be the other woman."

"Beth and I were headed for destruction a long time ago, Michelle. How I feel about you...that's something else entirely."

She didn't speak but leaned in just slightly toward my lips. All the wind had to do was shift...Just like the day of the wedding...And then, it was over. She pulled away slowly, until I was sure I'd imagined the moment.

"It's not that I don't care. You have to know that. I care. A lot." Her voice was shaking. "But you and Beth...That's one hell of a mess. And I can't go through what I went through with Charlie again."

So that was it, then. There was no mistake. What she'd felt was real. Our night was real. The energy that had been building between us for the better part of a year wasn't just some fantasy I'd created. And underneath that cool, unshakable facade was only a girl who was scared of getting hurt.

"I would never hurt you."

"You don't know that. You've hurt every girl who's come into your path."

"Ouch."

"I will not be the next one. I refuse."

"Is that what you think of me then?" I jumped to my feet, only then realizing how weak I still was, and gracelessly fell back to the couch. "That I'm just some dirtbag womanizer?"

"No." Her eyes grew sad with sympathy. "I think you just haven't found what you're looking for yet."

"You're what I've been looking for."

"I just can't let myself believe that."

But I was nowhere near ready to give up on her.

She left the room, returning a while later with my bagel on a plate and the bottle of Vicodin.

"Thank you."

"You're welcome."

"I'm feeling a little better today. I should be out of your hair in no time," I said lightly, feeling a little brighter than before.

"Too bad. I like you here."

My heart stuttered as she took my hand and ran her thumb across the top. "Shouldn't you be at work?" I managed to ask, once my breath came back.

"I should be, yes. But I have another patient I have to deal with right here. One giant pain-in-the-ass patient. She's a lot of work."

"You took the day off to take care of me?"

"Who else is going to make sure you don't fall on your face trying to get to the other room?"

"No one nags me quite like you do." I clenched her hand, never wanting to let it go.

CHAPTER TWENTY-TWO

B linding pain woke me from a sound sleep. It must have been the middle of the night, because even the streetlights were off. I sat upright in the dark, trying to rub some of the burning from my chest, but nothing was helping. I squinted down the hall to Michelle's room, but it was dark too. Reluctantly, I pulled myself off the couch and to the bathroom, where I fumbled through the medicine cabinet for something, anything, to take the edge off.

No Vicodin. Not even an Advil. I rubbed the burn again, but it was spreading to my back and through my shoulders. A light turned on somewhere behind me.

"Alex? Why are you up?" Michelle's voice was soft and immediately eased some of my discomfort.

"Just looking for my medicine."

"What hurts?" she asked, walking to my side and eyeing me all over.

"My chest. I didn't mean to wake you up. I was just trying to—"

"Oh, stop." She put her fingers gently to my collarbone and smiled. "Come with me. Let me take a look at it."

I followed her around the corner, surprised when she led me into her bedroom. I'd been in her apartment for days now.

We'd had countless meals in the living room. We'd cooked in the kitchen. Her home had become comfortable and familiar. But I'd never once been to her bedroom. Michelle kept the door closed most of the time, as if an invitation would undoubtedly mean sex. I hoped it would too.

"Sit," she ordered me, pointing to the bed. "And take off your shirt." Her professional demeanor kept me from cracking an obscene joke or making a come-on. Quietly, I did as she asked, pulling my white ribbed tank top over my head. For just a split second, Michelle the Nurse fell prey to Michelle the Sexual Being, and I caught her eyes falling to my bare form. Warmth colored my chest and my neck, temporarily numbing the pain I'd been feeling. "Looks okay," she said. "Still some bruising, but I don't think it's getting any worse."

"Tell that to my chest," I said, moaning.

"Such a baby. Does this hurt?" She raised a hand to the tender area just between my breasts and pushed, just slightly.

"A little…" My breath caught as the heat and silk of her skin brushed mine. Her eyes grew large, her hand wandering down my stomach. Her fingers feathered my skin until the blood had drained from my head.

"I put your pills in the kitchen cabinet so you could find them." She withdrew her touch. "I'll go get them."

I struggled to put my shirt back on, feeling cold and frustrated. Being Michelle's friend, forcing myself to sit there while she fought the need to be with me, was harder than I'd ever thought. A minute later, she returned with a bottle of pills and a cup of water. I took them from her as she sat on the bed beside me.

"Thank you."

"That should help." She smiled sadly at me, as if she'd just won a battle with herself that she wasn't sure she wanted to win anymore.

"I'm sorry I woke you up." I moved slowly toward the door. Leaving her was torture—especially when she looked so irresistible, wrecked with sleep, hair tousled, skin begging to be kissed.

"Alex…"

I turned back to her hopefully.

"You can stay…If you want…" I'd never heard her voice so unsteady and frightened. And I wasn't sure what she was more afraid of—me, or herself.

"Well, I…"

"That couch is awful." Her gift for indifference once again rewarded her with the composure she'd lost a minute ago. "Might as well get a good night's sleep in here."

I stood in the doorway, my feet sealed to the floor. One step in either direction would surely only contribute to whatever destiny we were headed toward. If I left, I could still save what I had of my heart. If I stayed, I was doomed for more pain when she inevitably pulled away again, like she always did.

"Yeah. Okay," I answered, like I was even close to strong enough to turn away.

She smiled again, a little more certain this time, and pulled back the covers to let me in. Instinctually, like I'd been meant for it my entire life, I drew her into me, cradling her body in mine, every inch of her pressed against me.

"How's your chest?" she asked, running her thumb up the arms that held her.

"Much better now."

She laughed. "I bet it is."

❖

The closer it came to bedtime the following night, the more anxious I got, until I was treading water in a sea of panic wondering whether I'd find myself in her arms again, or on the couch. That was the thing about Michelle really— you never knew what you were going to get. A trait that made many things exciting and unpredictable made evenings like this excruciating.

"I'm beat," she said with a yawn, and stood from her spot on the couch. "I'm going to bed." My heart began to pound as the panic escalated. Not knowing whether to stay or go, whether to ask her if I could follow or pretend the night before was a dream, I opted for sitting still, staring at her like a moron. She put her hands on her hips, staring back at me expectantly. Her lips curled into a slow, smooth smile. "Well? Are you coming?"

My mouth dropped open. I stayed glued to the couch for a second more and then sprang to my feet. "Yeah. Of course," I said, like we'd been going to bed together for years.

She lit a candle on the dresser and disappeared into her closet to change, leaving the door cracked just enough for me to make out the lines of her naked body cloaked in firelight. I watched her as I undressed down to my briefs and sports bra and slid under the crisp covers. She emerged in a soft-pink, silk cami that did little to keep her covered. Her bare legs peeked out from under a pair of lace panties. My muscles tightened. My breath became quick and hot. She was killing me.

Michelle climbed in next to me, making no effort to keep her legs from rubbing against mine as she did. My body tingled with the proximity, and the cold bed was suddenly burning hot. She lay on her side, one hand tucked under her pillow, and faced me.

"I like this," she whispered, pulling her hips closer to me and putting her hand on my naked thigh.

"Like what?"

"This. Sleeping with you." She ran her hand the length of

my leg now, trailing her fingers back down in soft patterns that sent sparks up them. I pushed myself toward her, willing her to touch me. But her hand stayed just a few safe inches away.

"Yeah. Me too." I tried to keep my voice steady, but it was cracking under the need beating through me.

"I have a confession."

"What is it?"

"I'm having a really hard time with this friends business…" She leaned forward and kissed me with a softness that painfully opposed the explosion building inside me.

"You are?" I shook.

"Yeah. I am." She kissed me again. "We don't have to rush anything, you know. Just because we're friends doesn't mean we have to…deny ourselves what we want…"

"It doesn't?"

Her tongue touched my lips.

"Of course not." Her hands lifted first my shirt and then hers. She pressed herself against me, her soft, full breasts brushing mine. I freed a small, scratchy moan and ran my hands down to her ass, kneading it as she ground herself against my leg. Her breath grew short. Her nails dug into my bare back, leaving what I knew would be marks for days. Something that sort of resembled the consequences for what we were doing flashed in my head. This is going to hurt, I thought. But then, the feeling of her naked body gliding over mine overrode my thought process. The feeling of her hands clawing at my skin, the feeling of holding her, and having her, even for the night, overwhelmed me.

❖

I woke up in the morning with her nearly on top of me. My legs were twisted around hers, and her hand rested on my chest. I smiled and ran my fingers up and down her spine while the midwinter sun shone in through the curtains. I'd never been much for cuddling. With Beth, with all of my past girlfriends, actually, I was quick to turn my back and fall asleep. But not with Michelle. Holding Michelle made me feel strong, and needed, and sexy. The sensation was powerful and raw. It gave me an energy I never knew I'd missed.

"You're better than any alarm clock." She grinned, opening her eyes and touching my face.

"Good morning." I couldn't silence the thought that I could do this every day, for the rest of my life. I felt crazy— absolutely fucking certifiable. I was dreaming of forever with a girl who wanted nothing more than a one-off screw and a friendship.

"Last night was fun."

Fun. Not my word of choice, but it was better than nothing.

"I have to go to work." She kissed me quickly on the mouth and got up to shower, leaving me feeling used and heartbroken, just like I knew I would.

I sulked the day away in front of the worst television programs I could find, eating out of a box of Cap'n Crunch and feeling pitifully sorry for myself. The end of the year was bringing with it the end of my marriage—my pathetically short marriage, which had probably been doomed from the start. It was hard not to mourn it. But Beth and I had ended long before we ever got married. We'd just managed to find enough good in it to keep us going for another few years.

And now, I was in love with someone else. I was in love with someone who was making me her personal sex toy and then calling me her best friend. I was hardly an innocent bystander, though. I took every flicker of her eyelashes and every brush of her fingers and ran with it, until the fantasy evolved into whatever I wanted it to be. I put my heart through the spin cycle every time she wanted me, but I did it anyway.

I'd never been this version of myself before. I'd never fallen so hard, so stupidly hard, as I had for Michelle. Nowhere even near it. When she wasn't around, I waited by my phone, mentally begging her to call or text. When she did, I threw myself a silent party in my head, like I'd just hit the jackpot and no one else could know. I thought about her obsessively, daydreaming about kissing her again, touching her again. She had more than penetrated my mind and my heart. She'd put down roots and moved in. And she didn't seem to be going away anytime soon.

In the past, I was the girl who made this happen. I made girls feel this way toward me, keeping them at a safe distance where I could never feel too much. Nothing was more important than what I wanted. But over time, I started longing for the tables to turn. I wanted to feel what they were feeling. I wanted to fall hopelessly, stupidly, in love with someone who made me feel vulnerable and weak, but also hopeful, and passionate, and alive. I was tired of safe. I just wanted to feel.

Unfortunately, once I found it—that kind of crazy, ridiculous love—it seemed to have forgotten to find me.

❖

"I've got Mediterranean," Michelle said, swinging the front door open.

"What the heck is that?"

"Food! Mediterranean food, you goof." She dropped two paper bags of takeout on the coffee table in front of me.

"They have a special cuisine? And here I was thinking

takeout was limited to pizza and Chinese." I smiled, my sullenness melting away every second I looked at her.

"See what you get when you're with me?"

"I get a lot more than takeout."

Michelle walked to the couch I was lounging on and sat down on my lap. Her weight against my body sent sparks through me, and I instinctively placed my face against her neck.

"You must be getting better. You're back to your suave pickup lines again." She rubbed the back of my head. I closed my eyes, overwhelmed by the need and the contentment that were all at once peaceful and unsettling.

"They aren't lines."

"Sure they aren't. You play that geeky lawyer card pretty well, but deep down you're just another smooth-talking hustler."

I laughed at her. "Hustler? Really?"

"Mmm-hmm. Hustler."

"So where's my fur coat and cane?" I loved to tease her.

"I believe you're thinking of pimp."

"Oh, right. Well, I promise you I'm neither."

Michelle placed her hands on either side of my face and kissed me, slowly, tauntingly, until my skin tingled and my blood heated. I itched to tell her how much I loved her—to tell her I'd waited my whole life to feel the way she was making me feel but never thought I could. For so long I'd thought I was broken, condemned to a life of searching for the greenest grasses. Not anymore.

We ate meat off skewers and drank wine at the dining-room table. After dinner, I washed dishes while Michelle waltzed excitedly around the kitchen with her glass of red, gushing about her heart-attack patient she and Natalie had ripped from the edges of death. There was nothing extraordinary about that night, or even about our makeshift life in her apartment that week. What was extraordinary was the thrill it brought. I'd never believed household chores and dinners and evenings we spent in could be passionate, romantic, full of that kind of storybook infatuation and long-term satisfaction. I thought I was incapable of these things. But now I'd learned that I'd just been incapable of them with anyone before Michelle.

While I scrubbed the last dirty plate, she came up behind me and put her arms around my waist. Her lips brushed my neck and the tip of my ear. I couldn't move.

"Meet me down the hall in five minutes," she said, her mouth trailing down toward my shoulders.

I couldn't speak, could only nod eagerly. She nipped my shoulder and left the room. My heart raced as I untied my apron and wiped my shaking hands on a nearby dish towel.

"Where are you?" I called, looking into her empty bedroom.

"In here." Her voice was coming from the bathroom, muffled by the sound of running water. I ventured slowly to the closed door. Beyond it stood Michelle, completely naked save for a coy grin. She blushed red when I entered, and I couldn't keep from looking her over. For a long time, I just gazed at her—her milky, round breasts that met her flat stomach, her sharp curves that ran down her hips, those long, firm legs that went for miles. Michelle wasn't the kind of girl you rushed with. No. Sometimes you wanted to, sure. But she deserved more than a quick fuck against a nightclub bathroom wall. Her body was art. I wanted to touch it, even when I knew I shouldn't. I wanted to understand it, even when I knew I probably never would. I just wanted to know it.

She took a step toward me, breaking the stillness between us. Her hands moved to my chest, and then she smoothed them over my T-shirt and pulled it over my head. She didn't say a word but just kissed me. When I was finally able to see beyond her breathtaking figure, I spotted the old claw-foot bathtub behind her that was nearly overflowing with white, frothy bubbles. A few candles were lit, but she'd left the lights on anyway, just to make sure I was looking at her. Her lips found mine again, this time pressing harder and moving faster. Slow guitar played on a stereo in the background as she unzipped my jeans, gently scratching her way back up my bare thighs. I gasped as she kissed down my neck and my chest, running the end of her tongue across my nipple. Heat flickered between my legs. I was as naked as she was now, as she took my hand and led me to the tub.

Michelle got in first, leaving just enough room for me to sit in front of her, her legs wrapping around me. The warm water pulled me under and her arms tucked me in. I let my head collapse against her chest, cushioned by the soft pillow of her breasts. She just held me, and I let every fear or care I'd ever had float to the surface and disappear.

❖

My broken bones and sore muscles had healed enough to lead to a serious case of cabin fever, but a part of me dreaded what my recovery would mean. My accident had sent me haphazardly to Michelle, and I knew my consequent rehabilitation would take me away. We were playing house. Michelle thrived in her role of caretaker, and I didn't hate being doted on, either. But when the bruises faded and the scars formed, I'd be alone again, without an excuse to need her—to have her. But I did need her. More than that, I wanted her. This went beyond any kind of dependence or rationality. In a short week there, as Michelle's live-in lover, I couldn't remember life before her. And I certainly couldn't imagine a life without her.

"How about we get out of here?" Michelle said, throwing open the door that night and hurling herself into an armchair.

"And go…?"

"Out! You must be going crazy in this apartment. It's been almost a week since you've seen the light of day. Come on, it'll be good for you."

"What did you have in mind?"

"My sister's boyfriend is in a band. They're playing down at Ginger's tonight."

"Are they any good?" I smiled as she got up and made her way to the couch, kneeling in front of me with her arms circling my waist.

"Terrible. But I promised her I'd go. And I'd really like her to meet you."

"You would, huh?" I pulled my hands through her long, thick hair that spilled down past her shoulders and onto her breasts, trying to keep my eyes from blazing a trail to everywhere I wanted to touch.

"I would."

"Isn't that a little…you know…coupley for you?" I was teasing her. She leaned in slowly and tugged at my bottom lip with her teeth, running her hands up under my shirt and down my back until my vision dimmed.

"Shut up," she whispered, nipping my lip one more time and pulling away.

"Okay, I'm in. Besides, I should probably get out of these sweatpants, anyway." Michelle grinned at me, the hazy glint of desire I'd recognize anywhere flashing in her green eyes.

"That's probably a good idea." In one smooth motion, she gently pulled at the sides of my pants, sliding them down slowly while she ran her tongue up my neck and to my ear, taking it in her mouth until my body writhed against hers. I took her head in my hands, holding her against me, willing her not to move—willing her never to move again. When I finally let her pull away, she kissed me again, harder, like she would never have enough of me. She pulled my T-shirt over my head, finally removing my briefs. Once I was completely naked, she stood up, unapologetically looking me up and down, her gaze burning me into a pile of unquenched desire. I wanted her to kneel back down, and when she didn't, I stood eagerly, the beautiful torture of wanting her so intense I felt it through my skin, in my bones, to my soul.

"No." She guided me back down to the couch. "I want you to watch me." I swallowed hard, my stomach cartwheeling into my throat. She stood motionless for a long time, seemingly savoring the need so evident on my face. I subconsciously ran my fingers up my bare thigh and my stomach as she unbuttoned her blouse. Her breasts edged out of the silk, barely contained by her white lace bra, and I reached up to touch them. "Just watch," she said softly, brushing my hand away. When she reached the last button, she let the blouse hang there for a minute, her milky-white skin peeking through like curtains hiding the perfect sunrise. She let it fall over her shoulders and to the floor, sliding one strap of her bra off, and then the other. The act was so sensual, so erotic, the muscles in my stomach clenched and I ached to pull her beside me. But sometimes, the anticipation is worth even more.

Michelle turned her back to me and pulled the zipper on the back of her tight pencil skirt, sending my mind reeling back to the night in the hotel in Boston. I reacted viscerally to the memory, my thighs tightening and my nails digging into the skin begging for some kind of relief. But it wasn't just my body that remembered. It was my heart. And I was once again reminded that this hold she had on me went far beyond anything superficial. It was more than flesh and heat and lust. It was so much more.

When she turned around again, she was naked, her eyes lit with just a hint of vulnerability that always made me want her more. I placed my hands on her hips, but she took a quick step back, shaking a finger at me. "You aren't listening very well, Alex. Don't you trust me?" She reached down and ran the finger over my chest, grazing my nipple. My breath caught, and I thought I might die before she let me touch her.

"I trust you."

"Good. Then don't touch." I slid my hands under me, as if they might break away from my body and disobey. Content that she once again had me in her grip, she moved forward, a devilish smile on her lips, and brushed one breast against my face, letting her nipple fall into my mouth, until she pulled away again, her smile growing by the second. She turned around, slowly inching onto my lap, her weight keeping my hands from running between her legs. All I could do was bite her bare shoulder as she moved her ass against me, the friction between us building so hot I thought we'd catch fire.

She got up and faced me, straddling my waist and forcing her mouth to mine so fiercely I couldn't move—didn't want to move. She kept my hands underneath me, teasing my mouth with her tongue until my breathing was harsh and I squirmed in my seat.

"Please. I have to have you." I pleaded with her.

"Where do you want to touch me, Alex?" She leaned back a little, her legs still wrapped around my waist.

"Everywhere." I gasped as she shifted against me.

"Here?" she asked, tracing circles on her tight stomach. I nodded dryly. "And…here?" She moved her hands up her body, pulling gently on her hard nipples and sighing.

"Oh, fuck. Yes. Please. There." I knew what was coming. And I wasn't sure I could sit still any longer. Not when my body was begging for release so badly one touch would push me over the edge.

"What about…here?" She slid her hand between her legs and my heart detonated. Her eyes were closed, and a small moan made its way past her lips.

"I can't. I'm too weak." Unable to take another second, I yanked my hands out from under me and pulled her against me until I was in complete control, allowing us both to tumble to the floor in a heap of sweat and limbs and bare skin. She laughed. "I succumb to your torture. You win. You can have whatever you want from me."

"Whatever I want?"

"Anything." She smiled again and pulled me on top of her, grabbing handfuls of my hair and guiding my head down between her legs.

"Oh my God, yes." She stroked the back of my neck, pulling me in farther to her as she moved under my touch. Her breathing built into heavy gasps until she was thrusting against my face. "Alex, I love you," she shouted.

I stopped, suddenly frozen, the flip-flopping of my heart rivaling the heat in my belly. "What did you say?"

She pulled out from under me, sitting up and bringing her legs to her chest. "I didn't say anything."

"Yes. You did. You said…"

"I didn't say anything, Alex. You must have been so into me that you're hallucinating." Humor was her best defense. But I knew what I'd heard. That was it. My sign. I couldn't give up on her.

❖

"Hurry up, we're going to miss the first band," I said playfully, coming up behind Michelle as she brushed her hair in the mirror and wrapping my arms around her. She closed her eyes and leaned into me.

"You feel good," she said with a groan. "Can't we just stay here and move onto act two?"

I turned her toward me and kissed her, my body igniting as if it too could remember the way we'd spent the last couple of hours…Tangled up, on the living-room floor, winter sunlight streaming in through the window to blanket her naked body.

"No. We have to leave the house at some point." I smiled and kissed her again. "As much as I'd like to become a shut-in with you and just fuck all day…"

"Mmm…so would I…" She rubbed against my leg and gently sucked on my neck.

"Hey." I gasped. "Stop that or we'll never get there."

"Okay, you're right. Just promise me there will be more of that later."

"Anytime, anywhere, baby."

❖

We took a cab to Providence and got out in front of a dark, dingy-looking bar with graffiti on the nearby sidewalks and guys in tight jeans smoking cigarettes at the door. The block was littered with twenty-four-hour Chinese takeout and broken-down newsstands. It was the kind of street you wouldn't want to find yourself alone on. The kind of street where you'd never expect to see someone like Michelle. This was what I loved about her. It was also what kept me mostly insane. Nothing was certain.

"There's Grace!" Michelle hailed a young, pretty brunette with her eyes, who was standing at the back door of the bar with a tall blond man in a leather jacket. She grabbed my hand and pulled me toward them, hugging her sister when we arrived. "I'm so happy to see you guys," she said, beaming, and squeezed the tall blond tightly around the waist.

"Alex, this is my baby sister, Gracie." I smiled and reached out to shake her hand. She hugged me instead, reminding me, distantly, of Auntie Judy.

"It's so great to meet you." Grace pulled away and looked me over from top to bottom, her wild grin growing as she did.

"Michelle…Why didn't you mention you had a hottie girlfriend?" My face flushed, but before I could say anything, Michelle took a step between us.

"Because," she said, "Alex isn't my girlfriend. She's just a friend."

Grace eyed her skeptically.

"Uh-huh. Well. That's really unfortunate for you, big sis." The two Masterses locked eyes, engaged in a conversation no one else could interpret.

"Hi, I'm Aaron," the tall blond said, extending his hand to me.

"Alex. Sorry, they must be terrible at introductions."

"Don't worry, I'm used to it. I'm Grace's boyfriend, if you can believe that, given her clearly homoerotic fascination with you."

I tensed a little, but then Aaron laughed, and Grace hugged him playfully.

"That's why I love him. He knows what a flirt I am. But he's the one I come home to every night." They shared a tender kiss, and Michelle and I stood there awkwardly.

"Will you two cut that crap out?" she finally said.

"Never. You're just jealous because you're single and bitter. And old," Grace retorted.

"I am not. Just single and old. But so not bitter!"

"So what about you, Alex? Do you have anyone special?" I could see tact ran in the family.

"Grace. Seriously?" Aaron looked embarrassed. "You don't have to answer that, Alex. These Masters women really don't know the meaning of the word inappropriate."

"I noticed." I put my hand on the small of Michelle's back, and she grinned shyly at me.

"Well, what do you say we head on in? Aaron, what time are you guys on?" Michelle asked.

"After this. I have to go set up, but I wanted to make sure I saw you before I did." He kissed Grace quickly.

"Good luck, baby," she called after him.

We flashed our IDs at the bouncer out front and headed in, easily finding a table in the nearly deserted dive.

"What do you two want to drink? It's on me." Grace got up and headed toward the bar.

"Beer is good," I said.

"Me too."

"Coming up."

"I forgot to warn you about my sister…" Michelle slid closer to me in the booth. "She can be a little…mouthy. Just don't listen to anything she says."

"Does your whole family come with a warning label?" I asked, putting my arm behind her. She smiled and cuddled up to my side.

"Just friends, huh?" Grace appeared again with three beers in hand, the familiar Masters smile on her face. Michelle pulled away quickly and sat up straight.

"Thanks for the beer," she said.

"Don't sweat it."

"Here they come!" Grace squealed and clapped her hands as Aaron and three other guys in various leather garments appeared on the small stage. He tapped the mic as if he couldn't be bothered to care and leaned in so close his mouth was touching it.

"We're Alien Turtle, and this song is called 'I Don't Care About Anything.'"

The drummer clicked his sticks together, and Aaron began mumbling into the mic to the rhythm of a couple of out-of-tune guitars turned up too high. Grace was glowing as she watched him. I recognized that expression. I'd seen it in Michelle when she looked at me.

Michelle kept her distance from me, at first, as the band played one bad Nirvana cover after another. But eventually she reached under the table and took my hand, stroking it with her thumb. It was a simple gesture, but something about being seen with her in public—without a complicated marriage or secrets or lies—sent my heart into a tailspin. I wanted everyone there to know what was going on between us. I wanted everyone to know I loved her, and I was pretty damn certain she loved me too. But then I remembered the reality of it all. I was just a friend. Hell, her sister didn't even know who I was. Maybe that's because I was nobody. Maybe that's because I didn't matter.

"I have to go to the bathroom," Grace said. "Michelle, why don't you come with me?"

"Sure, why not? You're okay staying here, right, Al?"

"As long as that creepy guy eyeing me in the corner stays there, I think I'll be fine."

They took off, leaving me alone with my beer and the undeniable thought that Michelle would never want me in quite the same way I wanted her.

Aaron's band played another four songs before I started to get concerned that something horrible had happened to Michelle and Grace. This wasn't exactly the safest neighborhood in Providence. And they were undoubtedly the prettiest girls here. In a moment of panic, I raced toward the bathroom and banged on the door.

"Just a minute!" It was Michelle. At least I knew some guy named Bart with a snake tattoo and a mustache hadn't kidnapped them. I was about to head back to the table when I heard their voices carrying through the door.

"Tell me the truth, Michelle," Grace said.

"I am telling you the truth. She's just a friend."

"So you aren't sleeping with her." There was a long silence, and I felt temporarily guilty for eavesdropping. But not enough to leave. "Liar. You are. You are absolutely getting it on. How long have I known you?"

"I don't know, since you were born?"

"Exactly. And ever since you started making out with Sarah Andersen in the ninth grade, I could tell when you were hooking up."

"What? That's stupid. How could you possibly tell?"

"I'm your sister. I just know you."

"Okay!" Michelle said, finally. "Okay, so we're having sex? So what? Haven't you ever heard of friends with benefits?"

"I'm sorry. I just don't believe you. I saw the way you looked at her out there. And that was not friends with benefits. Benefits, maybe...But there's no way you two are just friends."

"You're wrong." My heart sank a little and I started to go, but something about Grace's insistence kept me.

"No. I'm not wrong. Listen, Michelle. I'm only pushing you because I want to see you happy. I can't remember the last time you looked at anyone that way you look at Alex. Maybe never."

"So you're basing all of this on a look?"

"Among other things, yes. Just admit it. You have feelings

for her." There was silence again, and I pushed my ear against the door desperately.

"Fine. Yes, I have feelings for her. Is that what you want hear? I like her. Maybe even more than that." I fought the giddiness building inside me that made me want to run through the bar telling everyone she loved me.

"So what's the problem?" Grace asked, confused.

"It's not that simple. She's going through a bad breakup."

"That's it?"

"A divorce, actually…"

"And she isn't ready?" I wanted to break down the door and shake her. *I am ready, damn it. I've been ready for you my entire life.*

"She is. Or she says she is. Truth be told, I think their relationship was over long before it started. This split has been a long time coming."

"What is it then? Why can't you two just be together? Michelle, she's crazy about you. It's the most ridiculously obvious thing I've ever seen."

Why couldn't we be together? Why couldn't Michelle see that I'd never hurt her. She wasn't Beth. We were different. This would be different. I wanted to hug Grace for advocating for me. Maybe Michelle wouldn't listen to me, but she had to listen to her sister, didn't she?

"You don't get it, Grace. I can't just throw myself into the arms of a new divorcee who was married for a whole three years and seems to break every heart she's ever come across. That's suicide." *Ouch.*

"That's love."

"I can't. It's a death wish. You don't love Alex Harris unless you want to get hurt."

"She doesn't strike me as the player type."

"She's not. She's just lost."

"Well, maybe she's not anymore."

The sound of the faucet running drowned out their voices. I turned to head back to the table, but the door opened before I could get far.

"Alex. What are you doing out here?" Michelle asked.

"I have to use the bathroom…What else?" I shifted anxiously from one foot to the next and smiled, still trying to process everything I'd just heard.

"Okay." Michelle reached up and kissed me on the cheek, seemingly unaware I'd been an unknowing third party in their entire conversation.

After Aaron's band played their last song, Michelle, Grace, and I paid the tab and walked out into the cold December night.

"This was really fun. Thank you so much for letting me tag along. I haven't gotten out in a while," I said.

"Alex has been housebound for the past week. She got into a nasty car accident."

"Oh I'm so sorry! Are you all right?" Grace asked, tenderly.

"I'm fine, thanks. Your sister's been taking great care of me."

Michelle turned a hot red and laughed nervously.

"You've been staying with Michelle?" Grace's smile was clear, even on the dimly lit street.

"Just until she gets back on her feet," Michelle said.

"Well, I think that's wonderful. It was really nice meeting you, Alex." She hugged me again. "I really hope to see you soon." But she was looking right at Michelle.

Michelle and I walked a few blocks out of the neighborhood in hopes of finding a cab.

"I'm really glad we did that," I said, taking her hand in mine.

"So am I. I can't seem to get enough of you, Alex Harris."

"Michelle, stop."

She looked at me in surprise. "What is it?"

"This afternoon. When we were…You told me you loved me. I heard you." She turned away and started walking again.

"I told you, you heard wrong."

"No." I took her hand again and pulled her to a halt. "I didn't hear you wrong. You just about screamed it. Why can't you just admit it?"

"Okay. I said it. Are you happy now? People say all kinds of crazy shit when they're getting off. It doesn't mean it's true. Is that what you wanted to hear?"

"No. That's not what I wanted to hear, Michelle. I was outside the door when you were talking to Grace tonight. I heard everything."

She pulled away from me sharply. "You were spying on us?"

"No. Okay, yes. And I'm sorry for that. But you're avoiding the point. You admitted to her you have feelings for me. You admitted you're afraid."

"I can't believe you!" She stormed off several feet in the other direction, stopped, and turned around. "Okay. Okay, Goddamn it! So I have feelings for you? So it's not just sex? What do you want to do, run off and get married now? I'm not going to get hurt again, Alex. I'm just not. If you can't accept that, that's your problem."

I held her face and kissed her until I felt her body melt into mine. "I'm not Charlie. You aren't Beth. We aren't our pasts. We aren't our mistakes. Just think about that before you throw away a chance at something real."

Before she could say another word, she'd hailed a cab and got in. There was nothing left to talk about.

CHAPTER TWENTY-THREE

New Year's Eve: notoriously one of the most disappointing holidays in history. Twenty- and thirty-somethings get decked out in overpriced, skimpy black dresses, pay half of their month's salary for a cover charge, drink too much, and inevitably wind up puked on, crying, and broke in the bathroom of some overhyped club. I don't think I've ever met anyone who said, "My New Year's Eve lived up to every media-pushed expectation I had."

My holidays were never an exception. The only difference was, Beth and I had never bothered. Instead, we made it a point to stay in, with takeout Chinese, and watch whatever rerun marathon was being foisted on TV. Most years, we didn't even make it to the ball drop before we gave up and went to bed.

I was sure that year would prove to be no exception. Spending my Christmas in a hospital room hadn't set the bar very high. And, with Michelle's insistence on keeping things between us simple, I wasn't expecting much of this New Year's either.

Come the morning of the thirty-first, I was still playing the role of Michelle's platonic-roommate-meets-cuddle-buddy. My wounds, at least the visible ones, were more or less healed, save for some greening bruises and a newly formed scar above my right eye. But I still hadn't figured out my next move. Mr.

Watson had agreed I could come back to work after the new year began, but as of right now, I was functionally homeless.

I couldn't stay with Michelle forever…Could I? No. Of course not. Although it wasn't like I hadn't thought about it. What kind of lesbian would I be if I hadn't bought into the fantasy of a few broken bones leading to being nursed back to health, leading to some kind of undying love that prevented me from ever leaving her side? I wasn't any more immune to my U-Haul urges than most. But I knew that, eventually, begrudgingly, I would have to leave.

Michelle always left for work before I got up, careful not to wake me by slamming the front door. I spent the rest of my day reading up on my next case, drinking too much coffee, and counting down the hours until she came home again. When she finally did, she'd open the door, drop her purse on the floor, and walk over to me. She'd sit beside me, usually with an arm around me or some equally dizzying display of affection, and she'd ask me what I'd been working on all day. I'd tell her, excitedly, about the data I'd uncovered on the evil pharmaceutical giant that would right the wrong they'd done, and she'd listen attentively. She would tell me about her patient that threw a bedpan at her head, or the meeting she'd had that succeeded in keeping the city's oldest oak tree standing, and I'd beam. Then, we'd retreat to the kitchen, where I'd pour her a glass of wine and sit on a stool at the island while she cooked dinner. It was perfect—the everyday, routine existence suddenly thrilling and rejuvenating. The only problem was, it wasn't my life. I was just a visitor.

New Year's Eve morning she was gone by sunup. I opened my eyes to her cat, Tom, licking my nose, trying to fight the temptation to get used to this. Although she was falling asleep in my arms every night, she was holding tighter to her friendship resolve, throwing the walls up around her heart with moats and gates and guard dogs and whatever else it took to keep me out. So far, she seemed to be doing a pretty good job at it too. Maybe I'd never be able to penetrate her defenses. Still, I'd have rather been there than just about anywhere.

Something on the table next to me caught my attention—a white envelope labeled "open me" and a small ring box. I did as the envelope asked.

> *"In case I stand one little chance,*
> *Here comes the jackpot question in advance,*
> *What are you doing New Year's Eve?"*
> —M

My pulsed jumped as I reached for the tiny box. Inside were two white-gold cufflinks, a little tarnished from years of being loved hard by someone.

The harsh vibration of my phone against the table startled me, and I snatched it up. "Michelle." I looked around the room, as if expecting to see her, still reeling from the things in front of me.

"They were my father's. I thought you could wear them tonight."

"I uh…God, I don't know what to say…"

She laughed, apparently charmed. "Say you'll be my New Year's date."

Overstimulating, overhyped, overpriced, overrated, overdone New Year's Eve?

"Abso-fucking-lutely."

❖

Forget working. That was out of the question. It was hard to care about Martin Pharmaceutical's poor conduct when I couldn't stop thinking about Michelle. Instead, I puttered around the house—doing dishes, vacuuming, even trying to make brownies following a really easy recipe I found online—anything to keep myself occupied. Sometime after I'd given up and settled down to watch a special on TLC about a giant tumor, my phone rang again.

"Hello?"

"I guess it's time I give you some details, huh?"

"Why would you start filling me in now?"

Michelle laughed. "Your suit is in my bedroom closet. Put that on, make yourself pretty, and be ready to go at seven. I'll be there."

"Do I have a choice?" I felt great teasing her.

"Don't even pretend you aren't ecstatic. I have to go. Patients need saving. See you at seven, handsome."

Heat crawled up my cheeks, and a big, foolish grin bloomed on my face. "Later."

I ironed my shirt for a full hour, making sure I tackled every crease and made every corner stiff, following with what had to have been the longest shower of my life. I dried and combed my hair, and when that didn't work, I dried and combed it again. I fussed and picked until I was sure I looked as good as I ever would, all the while listening to Ella Fitzgerald crooning to "What Are You Doing New Year's Eve" on repeat. At 6:55, a black, unmarked car pulled up to the front door and laid on the horn.

Michelle's head was sticking out the sunroof as she hollered at me. "Let's go! We'll be late!" But her smile was brighter than the mostly full moon over her head. I hurried to the car, my wingtips slipping on the icy driveway beneath me. A graying man in a black cap and jacket got out and opened the back door for me.

"What's all this?" I asked, still in awe.

"It's New Year's Eve, Alex."

I'd never seen anyone look so gorgeous. Her long, loose curls I loved so much were twisted on top of her head, with rogue pieces making their way down and onto her shoulders, which were left naked and flawless by a long, black strapless dress.

As we drove, the headlights from passing cars highlighted her face, leaving the shadows a mystery I wanted to uncover. I wanted to stop time. I wanted to spend the rest of my life looking at her this way.

"I'm really glad you wanted to come," she said.

I reached across the warm leather seat and took her hand, still staring uncontrollably at her. "Are you kidding? Best invitation I ever had."

She offered me a smile latent with self-consciousness. "Did the cufflinks work?"

I answered by pulling up my sleeve to reveal the round, lustrous gold in the cuff of my white dress shirt.

"Alex, they look great." It was dark in the back of the car, but not so dark that I couldn't see the tears gathering in her eyes.

"Thank you. They're beautiful."

"I took them from my dad's room right after he died. They're the only thing of his I have. Everything else my mom could get ahold of she pawned for drug money. It means…" She took a deep breath, collecting herself. "It means a lot that you can wear them tonight."

Michelle leaned her head onto my shoulder, and I wrapped my arm around her. We rode the rest of the way in silence.

The car stopped, and the graying man opened the divider between us. "We're here, Ms. Masters," he grumbled in a thick German accent.

I still had no idea what we were doing. But I didn't care.

It was already the greatest night of my life. I got out of the car and walked around to the other side to let Michelle out, offering her my arm as I did. It turned out that Northwood Hospital had spent big bucks renting the State Room at the Bonneville, Northwood's oldest and most extravagant hotel. It was no surprise to me that Michelle hadn't told me details. She never did. But it didn't matter. I'd have spent New Year's Eve in a Dumpster if it was with her.

The hotel was packed with hospital employees, all dressed in their best black tie and all carrying around glasses of champagne. Several caterers in white were making the rounds with plates of feta-stuffed olives and cured meats. Michelle held on to my arm as we made our way through the crowd, a proud smile glowing on her lips like I was something worth showing. Maybe she thought I was.

She guided me to a table dressed with all white linen and perfectly polished silver, where the newly married Natalie and Charlie sat, nearly too wrapped up in whispering and giggling to notice us.

"Hi, love birds," Michelle chimed, finally breaking their trance. Charlie stood and took a step toward her, kissing her gently on the cheek.

"Michelle, I'm so glad you're here."

Natalie followed with a hug and a hello, as I pulled out Michelle's chair like the gentleman she'd trained me to be.

"Alex, it's so good to see you again," Natalie said, kindly.

"You too. How's married life treating you both?"

Charlie's face grew dark and shadowy as she spoke. "Oh, you know how it is. Don't you?"

A silence more uncomfortable than a crude joke in church spread over the table.

"I'm going to go find something to eat other than these little sorry excuses for appetizers," Michelle interjected.

"Natalie, why don't you come with me?"

"Gladly."

The two got up again, and I was left alone, staring into Charlie's once-kind, generous eyes that had turned cunning. She was quiet for a long time, eyeing me up and down like a protective father about to pull out his hunting rifle and chase me down the street.

"So," she said, simply. "You and Michelle."

"What do you mean?"

"Don't play cute with me, Alex. I know exactly your type."

I picked up my glass of champagne and nearly chugged it, wishing desperately for a waiter to come and bring another—just someone to get this nut away from me.

"My type?"

"Yes. Your type. Married, with who knows how many girls on the side. I don't care what you do with the others, but don't mess with Michelle. She's a very close friend of mine and Natalie's. And she's been hurt enough."

My blood warmed. "You would know, wouldn't you? Since you're the one who hurt her?"

Charlie was quiet again, her face softening and her eyes taking on a look of reverence and guilt.

"You're right. I did hurt her. But I'm not proud of that. And it's not like I was married to someone else."

I lifted my bare left hand out of my pocket and held it up in the air.

"I'm not married, Charlie."

"But…at my wedding I saw a ring…" she answered sheepishly.

I took in a long, steady breath, ready to explain what I hadn't even explained to myself yet. "I was married. Yes. But the rest of it you couldn't be more wrong about. I met

Michelle over a year ago. It's true, I was married to Beth still, but unhappily. We'd been over for a long time. Michelle and I were just friends. She was the best friend I'd ever had…" I twisted my hands together nervously. "But I couldn't help it. I fell in love with her. So no, there aren't other girls. There's just Michelle. I'm crazy about her, but I guess, sometimes, the right person comes along a little too late."

"Too late?"

"Yeah. Too late. You really did a number on her, Charlie. She just can't trust me."

"You love her?" she asked, glancing over my shoulder. It was the easiest question I'd ever been asked.

"More than anything."

She smiled at me, that big, charming grin that made it pretty easy to see why Michelle had been so taken by her. It took over her whole face and looked to come from somewhere far inside of her I couldn't really see. From behind me, I felt a tentative hand on my shoulder.

"Is that the truth?" Michelle's voice was soft and timid.

I stood, embarrassed, and turned to face her. "Well I, um…"

"We're going to go dance," Natalie spoke up, "aren't we, honey?"

"Oh, right. Dance. You kids have fun." Charlie winked, and we were alone. There were people everywhere, dancing and laughing and drinking and talking. But all I could see was Michelle. I looked down into her bright eyes and pink cheeks, her full, red lips that were formed into a subtle, questioning grin.

"Is that the truth, Alex?" she asked again.

"I guess that depends on how long you were standing there."

Her arms circled my neck. "Long enough."

"Of course it's the truth, Michelle."

"So then you," she teased the hair on the back of my head with her fingers, "you love me?"

I couldn't help the fire that was creeping up my belly and through my chest. It burned with a kind of unrecognizable, astounding tension that screamed at me over and over—*This is it. This is what you were waiting for. It does exist. And it's right here.*

"Maybe I do." I pulled her body against mine. "What's it to you?"

"Because." She put her mouth up to my ear, so close I could feel her hot breath against my skin. A shudder of want raced through me. "Maybe I love you too."

"You're everything." I took her face in my hands. "You're every dream I've ever had, everything I've ever wanted in someone. I have plenty of mistakes under my belt. But I swear to you, this time, I got it right. If you'll just give me a chance to—"

She forced her lips against mine. They moved eagerly and passionately, her arms clenched tight around me. When she finally pulled away, I was dizzy, the room spinning to the live brass band playing in the background. The other guests skirted around us, unaware of the moment that was unfolding—the moment that would carry us through the rest of our lives.

"I had to shut you up somehow." She smiled.

"It's always been you, Michelle. It's been you all along."

She kissed me again until my knees shook underneath me. "I love you."

And I thought about all the other times I'd been kissed—all the times I'd run. Then it came to me. I wasn't running from anything. I was running to it. Right to this moment—to this girl.

About the Author

Emily Smith was born and raised in a small town, where she started writing at an early age. She graduated from the University of New Hampshire with a BA in English teaching and went on to publish her first book, *Searching For Forever*, which pulled her headfirst into the world of creative writing. After years of working in medicine, Emily is currently in school becoming a physician assistant. She lives in Boston with her partner; their dog, Rudy; and their cat, Cecilia.

Books Available From Bold Strokes Books

The 45th Parallel by Lisa Girolami. Burying her mother isn't the worst thing that can happen to Val Montague when she returns to the woodsy but peculiar town of Hemlock, Oregon. (978-1-62639-342-4)

A Royal Romance by Jenny Frame. In a country where class still divides, can love topple the last social taboo and allow Queen Georgina and Beatrice Elliot, a working-class girl, their happy ever after? (978-1-62639-360-8)

Bouncing by Jaime Maddox. Basketball coach Alex Dalton has been bouncing from woman to woman because no one ever held her interest, until she meets her new assistant, Britain Dodge. (978-1-62639-344-8)

Same Time Next Week by Emily Smith. A chance encounter between Alex Harris and the beautiful Michelle Masters leads to a whirlwind friendship and causes Alex to question everything she's ever known—including her own marriage. (978-1-62639-345-5)

All Things Rise by Missouri Vaun. Cole rescues a striking pilot who crash-lands near her family's farm, setting in motion a chain of events that will forever alter the course of her life. (978-1-62639-346-2)

Riding Passion by D. Jackson Leigh. Mount up for the ride through a sizzling anthology of chance encounters, buried desires, romantic surprises, and blazing passion. (978-1-62639-349-3)

Love's Bounty by Yolanda Wallace. Lobster boat captain Jake Myers stopped living the day she cheated death, but meeting greenhorn Shy Silva stirs her back to life. (978-1-62639334-9)

Just Three Words by Melissa Brayden. Sometimes the one you want is the one you least suspect…Accountant Samantha Ennis has her ordered life disrupted when heartbreaker Hunter Blair moves into her trendy Soho loft. (978-1-62639-335-6)

Lay Down the Law by Carsen Taite. Attorney Peyton Davis returns to her Texas roots to take on big oil and the Mexican Mafia, but will her investigation thwart her chance at true love? (978-1-62639-336-3)

Playing in Shadow by Lesley Davis. Survivor's guilt threatens to keep Bryce trapped in her nightmare world unless Scarlet's love can pull her out of the darkness back into the light. (978-1-62639-337-0)

Soul Selecta by Gill McKnight. Soul mates are hell to work with. (978-1-62639-338-7)

The Revelation of Beatrice Darby by Jean Copeland. Adolescence is complicated, but Beatrice Darby is about to discover how impossible it can seem to a lesbian coming of age in conservative 1950s New England. (978-1-62639-339-4)

Twice Lucky by Mardi Alexander. For firefighter Mackenzie James and Dr. Sarah Mackenzie, there's suddenly a whole lot more in life to understand, to consider, to risk…someone will need to fight for her life. (978-1-62639-325-7)

Shadow Hunt by L.L. Raand. With young to raise and her Pack under attack, Sylvan, Alpha of the wolf Weres, takes on her greatest challenge when she determines to uncover the faceless enemies known as the Shadow Lords. A Midnight Hunters novel. (978-1-62639-326-4)

Heart of the Game by Rachel Spangler. A baseball writer falls for a single mom, but can she ever love anything as much as she loves the game? (978-1-62639-327-1)

Getting Lost by Michelle Grubb. Twenty-eight days, thirteen European countries, a tour manager fighting attraction, and an accused murderer: Stella and Phoebe's journey of a lifetime begins here. (978-1-62639-328-8)

Prayer of the Handmaiden by Merry Shannon. Celibate priestess Kadrian must defend the kingdom of Ithyria from a dangerous enemy and ultimately choose between her duty to the Goddess and the love of her childhood sweetheart, Erinda. (978-1-62639-329-5)

The Witch of Stalingrad by Justine Saracen. A Soviet "night witch" pilot and American journalist meet on the Eastern Front in WWII and struggle through carnage, conflicting politics, and the deadly Russian winter. (978-1-62639-330-1)